Respectfully Hated

VINCENT MCDANIELS

Copyright 2025 by Vincent McDaniels
ISBN 979-8-218-75063-3

Cover Art: 2Feet Productions
Elements of cover art sourced from artists on
123rf.com – batareykin;
standard licensing held by NEENALOVE INC.

2FEET PRODUCTIONS

2FEETPRO.COM

Books by Vincent McDaniels
Available now on Amazon.Com

Coming Soon

#4 In It To Win It
#5 Only On The Muck
#6 Links, Ties & Affiliations

Special "THANK YOU" to my powerline family who support me in all that I do. International Brotherhood of Electrical Workers – Y'all STAY SAFE!

To My Readers
I appreciate y'all taking time out of your busy day to sit down and read about how God brought me through 27 years and three months in the Florida prison system.

To all my brothers still behind that razor wire, don't give up. Keep fighting your case. I thought I would never get out as well, but what God has for you is for you.
Stay solid and prayed up.
Love y'all boys!

This book is dedicated to my mother,
Apostle Dorothy M. Fairbanks

Momma, I wish that you were here to see all that I have done.
I love and miss you so much.
You would be so proud of your son.
Rest in Heaven, Momma!

I want to thank, first and foremost, the Heavenly Father for giving me the ability to express myself on paper, in Jesus' name.

A special thank you to everyone who has supported my work from day one and pushed me and reminded me on numerous occasions to finish book three.

Windy Hill

Teresa Ward

Tanya Benjamin

Tamia Jones

Keyna Jones

Jorett Buckner

Ernetta White

Ronnie & Carla Felder

Tyrone & Stacye Anderson

Rev. Mark Shannon

Juwanna Myrick

Tonia Gilbert

Mary Teal

Octavia Evans

Clarissa Greenwood

Nadine Neal

Niecy Caster

Talaya Terry

Sabrena Harris

Rufus Mitchell

Salenthia Clayton

Jamie Kearns

Bubba Chuck

Lenny O.G. Red

Dexter Lee

Jose Oliviera

Billy Hilton

Dexter Tarver

Keo Nottage

Derrick Wells

Junior Ponder

Russell Byrd

Shambo V.I.

Brian Sanford GQ

Joe Francis "Soul Food"

Malik Mitchell

Sonya Wynn-Edmonson

The reason why people hate is because they lack what it takes to regulate!!!

-HELIMITE-
1994-1995
Appalachee Correctional Institution

Last but not least, a special thank you to everyone who has ever prayed for me, pointed me in the right direction, encouraged me, and constantly reminded me that GOD has a plan for me!

CHAPTER 1

I just got out of jail, Helimite, and I'm not going back," my child-hood friend Carrington, a.k.a Big Boy said as he sipped on his bottle of *Private Stock* beer while staring at me with his slanted Chinese-looking eyes.

"Jail?" I replied with a stunned look on my face. "You was in the detention center for 21 days, Carrington." He **hated** when I called him that.

"Stop calling me by my government name, Helimite."

"I will, Carrington. If you stop calling the detention center, jail, because we all know them 21 days in the detention center be 'sweet like candddayyyy,'" referring to the R&B group, Cameo's new hit song

The whole room erupted with laughter.

"So, stop trippin'. Plus, you know you still owe me a big favor for match making you up with my homegirl, Tara P."

I looked around at all the faces inside the Stoneybrook laundry room and said, "We gon' need at least three stolen cars and two of them need to be a Chevy IROC-Z in case we end up in a high-speed chase. I need Big Boy, Pus Head, and Spaghetti Man to get the stolen cars and meet up with me and Rufus at Tate's Gym at 8 o'clock tonight."

"Are you sure it's gonna be raining tomorrow, Helimite?

I looked to my left to answer Spaghetti Man. "The weather man on channel 12 says it's gonna rain all day starting at 10 a.m. and getting more severe after 5 p.m."

The laundry room goes silent for a half a minute then Rufus says, "It's gonna be a lot of guns to choose from, y'all. Please don't grab any 22's, Uzi's or Tec-9's because they jam up too much."

"We will meet back up behind Stoneybrook to split the guns up evenly," I added. I looked at Pus Head who was slowly nodding his head up and down as if he was still processing all the information. Pus Head acquired his nickname from the way his head was shaped. He had a few knots on his head that always looked like they were about to burst. Him and Spaghetti Man was tight as fish pussy and they specialized in B&E, breaking and entering. Spaghetti Man acquired his nickname from having long and lanky arms and legs.

Every one of us in the laundry room had become close friends through our times spent in half-way houses for juvenile offenders, Okeechobee Boys School and the Palm Beach County Detention Center. The only time we ever really came together on the street was for a caper, but this caper was a very important one. I was about to go to war with Hot Dog, which meant I was going to battle with his whole squad and Hot Dog was their fearless leader.

They had jumped me a week before at the New Edition, Force MD's, and Cherrelle concert at the West Palm Beach Auditorium. My injuries were not as bad as it could have been because I had tricked Hot Dog into a one-on-one fight, while his crew watched. But as soon as I started getting the better end of the fight, Hot Dog's crew rushed in to save him.

I inhaled deeply and rubbed my hand over my head and could still feel the lumps and knots from that night. My young, 16-year-old body was still aching. I still can't believe how stupid I was to go to that concert in the first place. It's normally the whole Stonybrook crew with me at big events but because this was a slow jam concert, I decided to go without the crew. You live and you learn, and I am grateful to God that I didn't lose my life that night.

My girlfriend, Nicole had been paging me and calling my mama's house constantly since that night. She wanted to see me and console me, I guess, but I wasn't about to let her see me in the state I was in, all swol' up like I was.

Big Boy interrupted my thoughts, "What about bullets, Helimite?"

I responded, "Pus Head can grab all the bullets and me, you, Rufus, and Spaghetti Man will grab nothing but guns."

The sound of music from a boom box was loud and clear in the air. We all looked to see who it was. My homie Eric Delk appeared. He was jamming James Brown, The Big Pay Back! Revenge!

And I must say, revenge was deep in my heart and mind for Hot Dog. It was clear that the days of having a man-to-man fist fight was over. It was all about the gun play now and if I had any intention on living to see 17, I had to get with the program and get my hands on some real fire power. As I tried to rock back and forth to the music in the background, it was impossible to do because my ribs were still sore from the beat down, I took.

The night of the concert, Hot Dog and his crew had every intention of ending my life. But thanks to the two random ladies, hollering and screaming, "Leave him alone. You're gonna kill him. The police coming," Hot Dog and his crew took off and ran. My classmate Aldric who was with me, suddenly, reappeared and he helped me up off the ground.

He said, "I ran to get some help because the two of us wasn't gonna be enough."

I responded, "Negro, let me go. You left me for dead," and I shrugged him off.

My neighbor saw me and gave me a ride back to the house where I cleaned myself up the best I could and went to sleep.

My mama hadn't noticed anything different in my movements and appearance. She was too busy working long hours at the RCA plant in Palm Beach Garden, and whenever she clocked out there, her and my stepdad, who I never got along with, didn't waste any time getting dressed for church. It seemed like they never left church. There was always a church revival somewhere, which meant they would be gone Monday night through Friday night. As much as they were seeking God's face, I was pretty sure God had our family covered in every way possible.

I couldn't share any of this beef stuff I was having with Hot Dog with my mama or my stepdad because I'm sure they would only want to pray about it, and this situation was beyond prayer to me. I had to reach out and touch Hot Dog with some hot lead since a fist fight was no longer an option.

CHAPTER 2

Calhoun Correctional Institution is located in Blountstown, Florida. That was 50 miles away from civilization, as I was told by the female property sergeant. She stood right in front of me with her hands on her hips as she began her orientation process with me.

"So, if you have any intentions on trying to escape from my institution," she proceeded. "Good luck to you because you're gonna need it."

Up to this point of doing time, I thought to myself, *it was almost unheard of for a black person to be planning an escape*. Now them white boys, on the other hand, be trying to escape every chance they get. They would rather get shot or killed trying to escape than walk around behind this razor wire fence for years at a time, being told what to do 24-hours a day.

I was sitting in a folding chair with all my property in front of me, half listening to Sgt. Pratt while four male officers stood by with their arms folded, trying to look as intimidating as possible. I received all this special attention because I arrived at Calhoun C.I. from Hardee C.I. solo, which raised eyebrows amongst the security here. They don't normally transfer just one person at a time unless the inmate had been involved in some type of scandal or an internal security threat.

I was pretty sure I would be released to open population once all my property was inventoried and I was checked by their medical department. I couldn't wait to let the sunshine bless my pale-looking brown skin and go to the canteen and buy a pint of butter pecan ice cream with a root beer soda.

Two of the four male officers standing by grabbed all my personal property that was in front of me and asked me to follow them to a nearby table that was flanked with three chairs. I sat down across the table from them as they began to remove my personal property from my bags. I sat there shaking my legs back and forth because of how cold it was in the building.

"Inmate Helimite, you shakin' already? You worried about something?"

"No, sir" I responded.

"You have any contraband in your bags, Inmate? Knives, drugs, anything?"

I looked at the officer and responded impatiently, "Not to my knowledge, sir."

Sgt. Pratt was ten feet away, heating up food in the microwave. It smelled good. She caught me looking in her direction and stated, "Inmate Helimite, what are you looking at?"

I responded, "Nothing, ma'am."

"So, I'm nothing or nobody in your eyesight, inmate?"

"No, ma'am. That's not what I meant. I was looking in your direction because I smell food."

I have been incarcerated for going on eight years now. The smell of a home cooked meal reminded me of the dinners my mom used to cook. I can just imagine my mama's Sheppard's pie and peach cobbler.

"Good answer, Inmate Helimite. I want you to keep in mind that we do put inmates in confinement here for reckless eyeballing female staff members."

"I understand, Sgt. Pratt," I responded.

"Inmate Helimite, why do you have so many pictures," one of the male officers inventorying my property asked, as he shuffled through a stack of photos that he pulled from a manila envelope.

We are not allowed to have nude photographs in the Florida Department of Corrections and this officer was making sure I did not possess any.

"A lot of my friends," I responded, "make a habit of writing me and sending pictures as well."

He held one photo in his hand and looked at it and turned it over to read the back and said, "Octavia is kinda cute."

"Yes, sir. She is." An eruption of laughter broke the silence.

"It looks like you were a very likable guy back in society."

I shrugged my shoulders and responded, "I guess."

The officer stated, "If you were so likable in free society, what brought you to my prison?"

I responded, "A bad decision, sir." And left it at that. I wasn't about to discuss my case with anyone other than my lawyer, who was still doing what he could to get me back to the Palm Beach County Courthouse. He filed a motion for correction of an illegal sentence. The Florida State sentencing guidelines had me in the 17-22 years guideline bracket for a second-degree murder charge and from 10-15 for the aggravated battery charge. The maximum amount of time Judge Miller was allowed to give me, under State sentencing guidelines in 1987 was a total of 37 years and not 55 years.

The appeal process was extremely slow. There were many inmates fighting their cases, attempting to recapture their freedom. No one wants to grow old or die in a prison, but the reality is that 60% of us will, or so the statistics say. I am hoping and praying that I don't end up being in the 60%.

"Inmate Helimite, you have a few items that you are not allowed to have at my prison."

I sat there thinking to myself that this was the second time this officer had said, "My prison," like he built it. I've seen his type before. This job is the best job he has ever had and with him being in his early 20's, he will make a career of it, make rank, and help all his kids, cousins, and friends get hired on.

"What items are you referring to, sir?" I asked.

"This P-35 can opener you have and this key lock. Only combination locks are allowed here."

"I'll mail it home, sir. I don't have any items I wish to donate to the Department of Corrections."

"Okay then. You have thirty days to send it home. Sign right here inmate." The officer shoved a document in front of me.

I read over the standard property form, which advised me that I had 30 days to mail it home, before signing. This clearly pissed off the two officers. I guess they wanted me to trust them and just sign my name, but I read the document, front and back before signing. I assumed they felt that I was being petty for one, mailing a can opener and lock home and two, reading the paperwork. It is what it is.

The officers escorted me to Medical for a quick check-up and then to my dormitory. Calhoun was a newly designed styled prison. It has three gun-towers on the compound. One at the entrance of the prison. Another one in between the center gates and the last one on the recreation yard, near the basketball court. It oversees the entire recreation yard.

Up to this point, I had not seen anyone here that I knew from back home or Polk C.I. or Hardee C.I. As I entered the dorm, the scent of bleach assaulted me. Somebody was dead serious about disinfecting this place. I was assigned to bunk #155, back row, next to a window. I took some baby powder out of my bag, sprinkled it over the mattress that was on the bunk, took my sheet and blanket and made my bed up, military style. I lay down to rest a bit before dinner time. Man was I tired!

CHAPTER 3

"The roof, the roof, the roof is on fire. We don't need no water let the muthafucka burn. Burn, muthafucka. Burn!" We all sang along to one of the very first songs I had ever heard with profanity in it. It was me, Fat Pop, Charlie Wine, Chik, and Gary. We were jamming to the music with four cane poles and four rod and reels hanging out of the back window. We were riding down the Beeline Highway, headed to our favorite fishing spot in Belle Glade, Florida.

I screamed out over the music, "My stomach is bubbling! We need to pull over somewhere so I can take a shit."

"Helimite, I don't know when you started cussin' but that's the second time today that I've heard you cuss. If I hear it again, I'm tellin' your mama," Fat Pop said. The whole crew busted into laughter.

It was get-away Saturday for us. Other 15-year-olds like me were at the Palm Beach Mall, shopping and trying to mack up on a girl. But here we were with at least 60 live crickets and four cans of wiggler worms headed for the 20 Mile Bend Canal. The canal is fed by Lake Okeechobee. Whenever the canal got low, we loaded a cooler full of drinks, two packs of bologna and cheese, two loaves of bread, and headed to Belle Glade. The only problem on this trip was that rain was in the forecast, but I haven't ever known rain to be the reason for fish not to bite.

My stomach was cramping. I knew it had to be that shrimp fried rice I bought, the night before, from the Chinese restaurant on 8th Street in Riviera Beach.

"I told you not to eat that mess, Helimite," Gary said. "You should have went to Dixie Fried Chicken instead. I know you heard about all the cats and dogs that keep coming up missing in the neighborhood. Them Chinese people catching them, dicing them up with seasoning and throwing 'em on the grill with that rice. All them cats and dogs that used to be around Snooks Bar are all missing."

I responded, "Stop lying, Gary!"

But he insisted that it was true. Chik looked at me and said, "Helimite, your ass might just start barking like a dog before the day ends." The crew broke into laughter again. I tried not to laugh because I was afraid that I might shit in my pants and if I did, they would talk about it and tell that story for years and years to come.

I tell Fat Pop again that I needed to go to the bathroom and that my stomach was bubbling.

"Hold it for five more minutes. We almost there now." Fat Pop was at least 22 years old. He was originally from Fort Pierce, Florida but had been living in Stoneybrook with us for some years now. Fat Pop had a car. He loved to fish just like we did, and he had a collection of porn magazines and porn tapes that made him 'the man' in our young eyes.

We entered a dirt road, and the ride became really bumpy. The unpaved road had holes here and there. There was a strong scent of smoke in the air. The workers from the nearby sugar mill had been burning the cane fields. It was 8:30 in the morning with a thick layer of fog still waiting to be burned off by the morning sun.

The four door Chevy Impala we were riding in finally came to a stop. I jumped out and told Fat Pop to open the trunk. I tore off a good amount of paper towels and headed to the tree line and bushes off from the canal. My seventh sense kicked in and I turned around to go back to the car. I grabbed the 12-gauge shot gun we always take with us to deal with the snakes and alligators that rule this part of the world. I had never used the bathroom in the woods like this before, so it was better to be safe than sorry. I've heard a lot of stories from the local people about Big Ben, the alligator that feasts on people and pets if you get caught not paying attention to your surroundings.

It felt good though to be back in our secret fishing spot where the bass and blue gills were always glad to fill up our five-gallon buckets. I moved with a sense of urgency, trying to find a good spot to take a squat and dump in the woods. I felt like I found the spot and looked around the area at least three times for snakes and 'gators. Satisfied with the area I chose, I relieved my system of whatever poison I had eaten. I started feeling better immediately. I constantly turned my head from left to right watching for wildlife.

To my right, the sound of a truck engine captured my attention. I looked in that direction and saw a light blue Ford truck. Some good-ole-boy country music was blaring from it, singing about a girl that had left him down and alone. The truck was headed right toward my crew. I watched as the light blue Ford came to a stop. Two white guys jumped out of the truck with handguns in their grasp. The driver was heavy set, about 5'8", brown hair and full beard with a red shirt and denim overalls on. The passenger was tall, at least six feet. He donned a straw hat, a blue t-shirt and faded jeans. Both men were aiming their pistols from left to right.

I heard the heavy-set guy shout, "What the hell you black rats doing on my land?"

Whatever was left in my gut flowed out like a river, more from fear than sickness. I wiped my ass and quietly eased my way back over to where my homeboys were. They were in deep trouble. I heard Fat Pop saying, "We apologize sir. We had no idea this was private property. We fish here all the time."

The heavy-set one continued, "Shut your fuckin' mouth, boy! And keep your hands in the air where I can see them. All you tellin' me, boy, is that y'all black asses have been on my property more than once. But today will be your last trespass. All four of y'all strip down butt naked."

The tall one asked, "Timmy, whatcha gonna do with their clothes?"

"We gonna burn them clothes and feed their asses to Big Ben!"

The tall one yelled out, "Yeehaw! That's gonna be a sight to see, Timmy!"

Fat Pop responded in the humblest voice I've ever heard him speak in, "Sir, I can't swim!"

"Boy, not my problem," the heavy-set one replied.

Charlie Wine and Chik were undressing and breathing hard with a look of frustration while Gary just stared in disbelief.

CHAPTER 4

The weather man's prediction was 100 percent right. It was raining cats and dogs in Palm Beach County the day of our heist. There were large puddles of water throughout Stoneybrook. My sister Teresa cooked chicken and rice. My baby sister Tanya and I had full stomachs. The closer it got to 8 p.m., the more nervous I got because my mama and stepdad hadn't left yet. They were taking forever to leave for church, which had me on edge. I had to show up for this caper tonight. My backup plan was to play sick and go to my room, lock my door, and jump out my back window. Now, how I was going to get back in, I had no clue since we lived upstairs.

Once I smelt my mama's favorite perfume in the air, a sense of relief came over me because I knew it wouldn't be long before they left. When the door to her bedroom opened, I was sitting on the couch watching T.V. She walked in the kitchen with her high heels sounding off against the kitchen floor.

"Teresa, put this food in the refrigerator and Vince, get in here and wash these dishes. Your sister cooked so you gon' clean."

"Yes, ma'am," I responded.

"Why you moving like you hurtin', Vince? You been playing that tackle football again?"

"Not lately, mama."

She was distracted once my stepdad came out of the bedroom and never got back to her line of questions.

"Mama, pray for me tonight."

She replied, "I pray for you every single day as I do for all my children, son. The devil is busy out here so it's a must to stay prayed up. You must seek God's face on your own as well, son. My prayers won't get you into heaven. You must repent of your sins and walk with Jesus."

"Yes, ma'am," I responded and proceeded to wash the dishes.

"Y'all stay inside this house now. We're headed to Fort Pierce for Paster Wesco's three-day revival."

Teresa responded, "Okay, mama."

Tanya gave mama a hug. I said nothing as I acted as if I was focused on my cleaning duties. I heard the front door close, and I sighed with a sense of relief. I looked at my li'l sister Tanya and told her, "Finish washing them dishes for me and sweep and mop the floor for me."

Tanya smirked at me and shook her head no. "Mama told you to do it."

"I know but I got something to do."

"What you gotta do? Mama said don't go outside."

I glared at Tanya and shook my head from left to right. She will tell on my behind in a heartbeat so I bribed her. "Tanya, I will give you five packs of Now-and-Later candies if you finish the kitchen and not tell mama I went outside."

I was going regardless. It was just easier to pay her off. Teresa wasn't going to tell because she had a boyfriend that mama didn't know about. I knew it, but I was **always quiet as kept** on that information because she was **quiet** about all my dirt. Tanya settled for the five packs of Now-and-Later. "Watermelon only," she said.

I agreed and hit the door. I had a pair of blue *Converse* tennis shoes on my feet, *Wrangler* jeans, and a blue North Shore High School sweatshirt. I was getting soaked as I took the path behind Stoneybrook for the half mile walk to Tate's Gym. I walked as fast as I could especially after hearing the train horn sound in the distance. I didn't want to get held up waiting on all them rail cars to slowly roll by. I broke into a slow jog and crossed the railroad tracks then slowed down to a walking pace again. The raindrops were cold against my face. I could hear the train rolling behind me and I crossed the softball field at Tate's Gym.

We called Tate's Gym the sweatbox because there was no air conditioning. All exit doors stayed open to allow the air to flow through the gym.

I learned how to perfect my basketball skills in this gym and I won my very first basketball trophy here. I met Muhammad Ali here as well. How had my life come to this? I possessed so many talents and gifts, but talents and gifts are of no use to me if I can't stay alive to use them. Tonight was all about survival and only the strong will survive.

"Helimite."

I turned to my right and saw Rufus with a rain jacket and jeans on. He had a Denver Broncos book bag next to him.

"Rufus, why you got your school bag with you?"

"We gotta have something to put the guns in and feel this," he held out the bag to me.

I grabbed the bag. It had some weight in it already. "What's inside?" I asked. He unzipped it and showed me three red bricks.

"What's them bricks for?"

"To break the glass on the display cases once we inside. It ain't like we got a key, Helimite."

"You dead right!" I responded. "Good thinking, my dog." We give each other a hand slap. "Where the cars at?"

Rufus shrugged his shoulders.

"It's about 7:45 right now. I hope them fools ain't out joyriding knowin' we gotta handle this caper."

Ten minutes later, two IROC-Z's and a Monte Carlo pulled up to the gym. Me and Rufus walked up to the cars. Big Boy was driving an IROC-Z and Spaghetti Man was driving the other IROC-Z. Pus-head had the Monte Carlo. The rain was still pouring down, so I asked everybody to jump into the Monte Carlo.

Once everybody was in, I went over the plans again. "Once we get to the gun shop, we're going to the back of the shop and running this Monte Carlo straight through the wall. Pus-head, you gonna crash through the shop wall in reverse. Once we in, Rufus got three bricks to break the glass display cases that all the guns are locked in. Pus Head, all you grabbin' is the bullets. Everybody else knows what to get. If we get into a highspeed chase, we will split up and meet back up behind Stoneybrook."

The sound of the rain was loud, beating on the roof of the Monte Carlo. I finished off by telling everyone, "If I don't see you or you don't see me at Stoneybrook by midnight, you know I'm in the Palm Beach County Juvenile Detention Center. *Quiet as Kept.*"

CHAPTER 5

A Latin looking inmate entered the dormitory and sat on the bunk right next to mine. He asked in his best English he could muster up, "My friend, you have a cigarette?" This inmate doesn't know me from a can of paint but felt comfortable enough to call me friend.

I told him, "Me no smoke," in my best attempt at sounding Spanish.

He responded, "No *comprende*. Me no understanding English, my friend."

I laughed and nodded my head up and down. Before anymore words could be exchanged, the P.A. system came to life and announced that the yard was being called for count. "All inmates are to report back to their bunks for count."

I propped up my pillow, laid back, and watched all the inmates assigned to this dorm roll in from the recreation yard. Two guys entered talking loudly, back and forth, in a heated debate pertaining to the Detroit Pistons and Chicago Bulls upcoming game. The way these two inmates looked, you could tell their whole afternoon had been on a basketball court. The knee braces, the high dollar tennis shoes, and their sweat-soaked t-shirts, they were a dead giveaway that they had been ballin' all afternoon. One of the guys looked familiar but I couldn't recall where I knew him from until I heard the other inmate he was debating with call him, "Black Mike." Black

Mike earned his simple nickname from having charcoal black skin and Mike being his first name. He was also known as Black Jesus because he is known to be the truth and the light and the gospel with a basketball in his hand.

This cat was from the White House projects located in West Palm Beach, Florida. The White House Projects was the Stoneybrook crew's biggest rival, not for sports but for violence. We fought the White House Gang wherever and whenever. The most memorable clash was inside the Palm Beach Mall in 1985. I still can't believe the amount of destruction we, as juveniles, had done inside that mall. I can still remember the shop owners scrambling through clothing stores and jewelry shops trying to roll the shutters closed and secure their establishment. We had no intentions of robbing or stealing anything. We were out for blood through straight up fist-fighting.

The sound of the P.A. system interrupted my thoughts as the officer informed everyone that it was count time. "No talking. Sit in an upright position for count. It is now count time."

I sat in an upright position for count while two male officers walked through the dorm to count. Once they finished, one of the officers' shouted, "Relax!" Everyone laid down, at this point, to wait out the count process. At least 1,300 inmates needed to be accounted for before we could be released for dinner. I was still tired from my trip to Calhoun from Hardee C.I. I was expecting the transport officers to stop and do a layover at one of the neighboring prisons along the way but that never happened. My ankles and wrists were still sore and swollen from the shackles and handcuffs that had been tighter than usual. I guess they wanted me here at Calhoun ASAP. I was Inspector Queen's special delivery.

The P.A. speaker sounded again that count was clear. I walked to the bathroom to wash my hands. The smell of bleach was still present in the bathroom. This was a good sign because normally a prison bathroom smelt like piss. Whoever the orderly was over this bathroom was on-point. I finished washing my hands and took a seat in the T.V. room. The T.V. was tuned to a Tallahassee news station talking about how the farmers in the area needed rain for their crops. I was sitting there thinking to myself, *Helimite, ain't nobody coming to visit your ass way up here in Blountstown, Florida. You thought you was far away from home at Polk C.I. and Hardee C.I. Boy, you in the Florida panhandle now.*

I got up and walked to the water fountain for a drink. The water was extremely cold to the point that my teeth hurt. What hurt even more as I looked around at all these different nationalities of life present in this dorm, was not knowing when all of this will actually come to an end. My mama always tells me when we talk, "Son, this too shall pass. Trouble don't last always." But when, is the question!

"Chow time. Chow time," the P.A. system barked. "You have exactly five minutes to depart the dormitory."

I took a quick look at the Department of Corrections menu posted on a bulletin board in the T.V. room. It read, to my disappointment, beef stroganoff, green beans, cornbread, and applesauce. I had a locker full of food – cans of tuna, peanut butter, and honey granola bars. I was not about to eat beef stroganoff, mainly because it was not beef that was being served in the Florida prison system anymore. They had come up with a mystery meat because of budget cuts. Someone somewhere was pocketing that money now.

Since I was at a new prison, I decided to go ahead and take that walk to see who I might know. More importantly, I wanted to see how many women work here. If you show up to a prison with hardly any female officers or staff, that is a prison no real man wants to be doing time at. The sight of women, for me, was a reminder of the femininity that awaited me once my freedom was restored. On the flip side, I'm Helimite so I need to look things over to see what my next girlfriend may look like. *Quiet As Kept.*

We lined up in a single file line and took about a 60-yard walk to the chow hall. The line was long, and it was a warm day. I looked down at my *Guess* watch on my wrist. It was 5:21 p.m. As I stood there, I recognized a few faces but no one that I had a bond with. I said nothing. *Quiet* and observant. Once I finally made it inside the chow hall, the heat was undeniable. Sweltering. Sticky. Heavy. The ceiling fans were unable to cool the mass number of bodies inside the chow hall. Even though the food was being served, I couldn't smell it. It was probably due to the cooks being unable to use seasoning on the food.

There were officers everywhere shouting and pointing at inmates and advising them on where to sit. One sergeant yelled out, "Less talking and more eating! Row one! You have three minutes." The sergeant had a pot belly and was sweating like someone had thrown water on him. He had a brown washcloth and used it to constantly wipe his face to keep the sweat from dripping into his eyes. The flies were visiting every table before being swatted away. Up to this point, I couldn't help but notice that there weren't any black officers anywhere in sight. It made sense, I guess, considering where I was located. Blountstown, Florida is in the panhandle. 200 miles from Mobile, Alabama in the west and 50 miles from Tallahassee, Florida in the east. I hadn't laid eyes yet, either, on an officer that didn't act or look professional. This was my third prison, and I was still at the front end of this 55-year sentence.

I grabbed an empty tray that was still wet from the dish washer. I began the slow walk through the serving line as my empty tray took on weight from all the food that was added to it. I still had no intention of eating any of it. I grabbed a cup near the end of the serving line, and I followed the inmates in front of me. We were all instructed where to sit by security. It's four to a table. As I looked around my table at the other three inmates sitting with me, their heads were down, feeding their faces like they were at *Red Lobster*. You should have seen the looks of disbelief on their faces when I said, "Anybody want this tray?" Hands moved like Flash Gordon.

I left the tray with them and walked toward the drink cooler with my cup in hand for a drink of sweet tea. It was rumored throughout the prison system that if you drank the tea for a good number of years, it caused your penis to not be able to rise to attention in the heat of desire. I really didn't believe it, but I took heed to all the stories I heard from convicts who had been in the system way longer than me. I tasted the tea and placed my cup in the dishwashing window. As I turned to leave out the door an officer stopped me and asked, "Where's your tray?"

I answered, "I gave the tray away, I'm allergic to mystery meat."

He impatiently looked at me and said, "Boy, this probably the best eating you've had in front of you your whole life so, stop complaining and go back out there to the dining area and bring me back a tray to put in this here dish room."

"I gave the tray away, sir," I responded.

He scolded me, "Boy, that there is bartering and can get you 30 days in our hot box confinement. So, unless you wanna spend 30 days back yonder, go get that tray."

It was my first day at Calhoun and they already with the bull. I just spent months in confinement, and it was my first day back into open population. *Helimite*, the voice in my head screamed. *Take your stupid ass back to that table and get the tray and keep it moving* and that's exactly what I did then left the kitchen and walked toward the recreation yard.

CHAPTER 6

I was standing 20 feet away, behind Fat Pop's Chevy Impala, watching the scene as if it were a movie. The heavy-set white guy who had been pretty much doing all of the talking and directing yelled, "If y'all boys wanna make things right with whatever God you serve, the time to do it would be right now." At that point, I had seen enough and heard enough to know that my homeboys were about die.

Fat Pop and everybody else screamed out, "Helimite, where you at?"

The heavyset white guy laughed a wicked laugh as if he was possessed by some type of evil spirit and said, "Helimite! Now that's gotta be some new negro religion that's come out. Y'all nigger black rats have completely disrespected Jesus-fucking-Christ's name by serving a false God – Helimite!"

With every ounce of boiling blood within me, I stepped from behind the Impala and pumped the shotgun, adding a shell to the chamber. "Y'all hillbillies drop them guns now or you will die right where you're standing."

The tall lanky guy dropped his gun immediately and raised his hands in the air. The heavyset guy was clearly shocked at how the tables had just turned. He was trying to regain his composure but still hadn't dropped his weapon. He was breathing a whole lot faster now. All my homeboys dropped their arms to their sides with a look of relief on their faces. Chik moved to pick up the handgun that the tall lanky guy had dropped to the ground. The heavyset guy growled, "I *hate* that your black ass has the ups on me right now, but I must *respect* that shotgun you holding on me." At that point, he dropped his handgun.

All my homeboys were completely naked. They moved forward to get the weapons and their clothes. We took possession of the handguns. One was a 357 Magnum, and the other was a 38-snub nose.

"Let's go y'all," Charlie Wine said. The rest of the crew began to gather the reels and rods and cane poles we came with. The heavyset white guy raised his voice again, "That's right. Get gone and consider your black asses lucky today."

I raised and pointed the shotgun at his head and in a low voice, not quite a whisper, I ordered the heavy-set guy, "Get naked and get your fat ass in that canal."

"You too, dude," I said to the tall lanky guy.

"Helimite, let it go!" Chik said.

"Hell naw. This eye for an eye treatment. They was gonna feed y'all black asses to Big Ben, the alligator so let's see if Big Ben like white meat."

"Helimite, you done went crazy," Fat Pop said. "Let it go!"

"It wasn't crazy ten minutes ago when they was about to send y'all out there," I responded. "So, fuck them!" I turned my gaze to the two white men standing ten feet in front of me, "Get y'all asses in that water right now," I screamed. "Ain't no fun when the black rat has the gun."

They both entered the water and swam like they were in a race trying to reach the other side of the canal, which was a good 60-yards, at least. We took their clothes with us. Gary flattened all their tires, and we piled back into the Impala and started back down the path headed to the main road and then on to the Bee Line highway to get back home.

Gary asked, "Helimite, what took you so long to come?"

"Man, I was still shittin'!" I responded. "Y'all better be glad I had to shit and took the shotgun with me. My mama always said that everything happens for a reason, so be grateful for the things you can't understand or happen in your life."

As Fat Pop drove, he constantly looked at the rearview mirror. "Pop, ain't nobody following us or chasing us. We flat all their tires. They butt ass naked with no clothes to put on. They probably still trying to reach dry land. Relax," I said.

"Hell naw! Keep haulin' ass, Pop," Charlie Wine said.

As we rode back to Stoneybrook, I was in deep thought and every-one else in the car was silent as well. I replayed everything that just happened. I had seen on T.V. and heard about encounters in the past about the KKK or angry white people out and about, looking for an opportunity to hurt someone with skin color opposite from their own. With the exception of Fat Pop, every person in the vehicle was either 14 or 15 years old. This incident would shape and change all our lives and how we viewed white people, and the way that we moved around them forever.

Chik was seated next to me in the back seat and yelled out, "Hey Pop. Turn some music on!" The Alpine sound system roared to life with the rap song, *The Message* by Grand Master Flash and the Furious Five.

Don't push me
'Cause I'm close to the edge
I'm tryin' not to lose my head
It's like a jungle
Sometimes it makes you wonder
How I keep from going under

All five of us were rapping the lyrics along with the song, giving each other hand slaps. What I didn't know in that moment was that it would be my last fishing trip with my childhood friends. Myself and Chik would follow the pattern of what other teenagers were doing on the weekends – Palm Beach Mall to shop and play video games and chase girls.

CHAPTER 7

My heart rate was starting to pick up as I got into the Iroc-Z with Big Boy. Rufus got in with Spaghetti Man. Pus-Head was solo in the Monte Carlo. A big boom of thunder sounded off, loud enough to wake the dead. Where there's thunder, lightning will always follow and that, it did. The street we were on, Blue Heron Boulevard, lit up like a football field from the bolt of lightning that streaked across the sky. We made a left on Old Dixie Highway, headed toward Silver Beach Road.

Big Boy was somewhat of an expert get-away driver. When he was 14, he used to steal fast cars all the time. He would find a police car and draw attention to himself by burning rubber or running a light to get the police to chase him. Big Boy was a fool, but he was my main man when it came to any kind of violence, along with Rufus. Big Boy had shot another kid at Watkins Jr. High School and was kicked out of the public school system in Palm Beach County.

I wanted to break the silence in the car, so I asked, "Big Boy, you still talking to Tara P.?"

He smiled and did the crazy laugh that he does and replied, "Yeah, Helimite. I think she really likes me, dog."

I shook my head and laughed as I thought about how violent my partner was but was as shy as a kitten when it came to a girl. The way Big Boy and I had become partners was crazy. He was from the Fire House neighborhood in Riviera Beach, located right off 8th Street. I never understood why they called it the Fire House, and no one ever defined the reason or how it got that name.

On the day we met, my mother had six loads of dirty laundry that needed to be done and took me with her so she wouldn't have to carry those six heavy loads of laundry in and out of the laundry room. We went to the laundromat right off Old Dixie Highway, next to the Fire House neighborhood. I had a pocket full of quarters, playing the video game Space Invaders and I wasn't doing well at all. When the game ended, I switched to Ms. PacMan. Big Boy walked in, looked me up and down, and watched me play. When the game ended, I reached into my pocket to insert another quarter.

Big Boy said, "Hey man, I got next on the machine."

I told him, "I ain't through playing yet."

He said, "Get off the machine, man, before you get beat up in here."

I looked back over my shoulder at my mama who was reading the latest issue of Jet magazine not paying me, or this situation, any attention. I told him, "If you wanna fight, I ain't scared to fight you but let's go out the back door and do it outside."

Big Boy looked at me and said, "It didn't start outside but bring yo' skinny ass on out this door."

We walked through the back door. No words were exchanged. Big Boy bum rushed me and went low, scooping me off my feet and slamming me onto my back. He was on me like a fly on food. I kicked both of my legs furiously in an attempt to get him off of me. One of those random kicks ended up hitting him in the groin area and brought his display of violence to a halt. As he reached for the area of pain, it was my turn to unleash an undisclosed number of left hands and right hands to his head. As I drew back my right hand to strike Big Boy, yet again, someone grabbed my arm and yanked me off him. To my surprise, it was a Riviera Beach police officer. They were riding by, I guess, and spotted us in battle.

They helped Big Boy off the ground, "Carrington, seems like you finally met your match."

Carrington, a.k.a. Big Boy, laughed his stupid laugh and said, "That was only round one. He gotta fight me every time we see each other."

The big white officer, who everybody on the street had nicknamed Curly Top because of his hairstyle said, "If I catch y'all fighting again, I'm taking both of y'all to the juvenile detention center."

I nodded my head up and down and entered back into the laundromat. Even with all that had taken place outside, my mama was still in her seat, reading her magazine. I went and sat by her to gather myself and to listen to the radio that the laundry attendant was playing. It was on Soul16 WPOM. The DJ played a song called, *It's Like That* by Run DMC. Big Boy came back in and got on the Ms. PacMan machine and looked over his shoulder every now and then, only to see me helping my mother move clothes to the dryer.

After I finished helping my mama, I walked over to where he was and the first thing out of his mouth was, "Where you from?"

I responded, "Stoneybrook."

He looked at me with his head slightly tilted, side eyeing me and asked, "That's where you learned how to fight?"

I said, "A little bit. We have to fight all the time in Stoneybrook, man. It's like that and that's the way it is!"

CHAPTER 8

The recreation yard at any and every prison you go to was where everything went down. In my opinion, it's the most dangerous spot inside the prison. Too many people with too much time and a lot of frustration and issues that could range from just about anything are all in one place. At the same time, if you decided to play any kind of organized sport or weightlifting, it could be an outlet for releasing steam, stress, or pressure you might be feeling.

I bumped into this brother named Neal. I used to play ball with him back at Polk C.I. He shook my hand and started a line of questioning about good ole Polk C.I. days. What year did I leave? Was fine-ass-Ms-Jackson still working there, etc.? Once he got the answers to his questions, I started my own line of questions about my present situation at Calhoun C.I. I was not interested in what happened in the past at Polk.

Question #1, is there any weed on this compound? If so, how much is an ounce? Whatever that number was will tell you if the hustle will be worthwhile or not. Being this far up north, everything was going to be more expensive because drugs were harder to get. An ounce of good weed is priced at $800 dollars an ounce.

Me and Neal walked the track on the rec yard where all the joggers were blowing past us, getting their miles in for the day. I looked through the razor wire at all the trees surrounding the prison. Leaves were blowing in the wind and in that moment, I wished to be in that wind being blown away from this place. So much of my time was spent hoping and wondering when all of this would end. I took a deep breath and sighed at how the best years of my life was being lost to the prison system. Whenever I felt like this, I knew it was time to call and write my mama. She always directed me on what scriptures I needed to read to get through moments of loneliness and despair. The air was crisp and clean out here in these woods. I continued my walk and contemplated what my next move should be.

I know it sounded crazy because I'm in prison and it is a controlled environment. It is not like I have a whole lot of options, but I know if I am going to be here, I needed a good job in the air conditioning, working for or around women. It was enough already having to live with a bunch of men. My workspace, if I can help it, should be softer and colorful, and more sensitive to my needs. It was apparent that the doctors, nurses, and secretaries do not get the same training as officers do. From my experience, the majority of the officers I had encountered were all about security, discipline and control. The Medical Department was geared toward helping and healing. Caring was their trained mindset. It was in my best interest to figure something out.

Neal broke my chain of thought when he mentioned that two weeks ago Calhoun C.I. had experienced their first riot. I raised my head and asked, "Riot?"

"Yeah, Helimite. It was ugly."

Neal continued, "The riot wasn't inmates versus inmates. It was inmates against the police. The inmate population was frustrated with the conditions they were being subjected to and the level of pettiness of the police staff."

I was highly interested in Neal's story and slowed down my walking pace to look at him.

Neal continued, "So, the inmates snapped and started kicking the police ass. They had to call in the National Guard to regain control over the institution and situation. But by the time the National Guard arrived, the damage was already done. Eight staff members were transported by helicopter to outside hospitals for all kinds of injuries."

A riot? I thought to myself. I had to add that this is something that I have to be prepared for behind these razor-wired fences.

"One thing about a riot, Helimite," Neal continued, "…is we outnumber the police at least fifty to one until backup gets here. Once they get here, the joke is over. They spraying mace, kicking ass with K9's barking and slobbering out their mouth, looking for an opportunity to bite anyone that's going against the grain."

The prison P.A. system came to life. I was shocked when the voice asked for Inmate Helimite to report to the Security Building immediately.

Neal grimaced at me and asked, "Helimite. What them white folks want with you already?

I shook my head and said, "Your guess is as good as mine, Neal. Where is the Security Building?"

"Up front by the visiting park."

I gave Neal a hand slap and told him, "I'll be back to dunk on your tall ass in a minute."

He chuckled hard and responded, "Not happening, Helimite!"

Neal was 6'8" with hands two times the size of mine and, as I remember, Neal only played basketball for the highest bidder. Everything is a hustle in prison. I walked across the recreation field and stopped for a minute to watch the Latino brothers play soccer. These inmates were in their own world, bumping into each other and running constantly behind that soccer ball, cussing and grunting the whole time.

The P.A. system came to life again repeating, "Inmate Helimite, report to the Security Building."

I kept it moving in that direction. When I got to the entrance gate of the recreation yard, I told the officer standing there that I needed to report to the Security Building.

He asked me, "What for?"

I told him, "I don't know. They paging for me to report there."

He asked my name. I tell him, "Helimite."

He gets on his walkie-talkie to verify what I just told him. He looked me up and down and directed me to tuck my shirt in. "Where's your belt?"

"I don't have one, sir."

He shook his head from side to side and stated, "You don't need one where you're going anyway."

When I arrived at the Security Building there were two officers already waiting to escort me without handcuffs, which was a good sign to me that I didn't do anything wrong. Wait a minute. A sense of fear took over me. Has something like a death in my family occurred? The captain might be delivering the bad news since the Chaplin has left for the day. My mind was all over the place as I entered the small beige and brown colored office. Walkie-talkies were resting on their chargers and a small computer was sitting on his desk.

"My name is Captain Riggs," he said with a curious look on his face as if he were trying to figure something out. He had brown hair and a handlebar style mustache. "Inmate Helimite, you are being transferred to another institution per Inspector Cook's orders. Apparently, your involvements back at Hardee C.I really pissed off Regional Inspector Queen to the point that she called our Inspector with an ear full about your supposed illegal involvement with staff back at Hardee C.I. Inspector Cook is convinced that you wouldn't be a good addition to our population here at Calhoun."

I stood there listening to this bull-junk thinking *show me what a good addition to a prison population looks like. I mean, we're all criminals, right?!* At the same time, I had no say in this decision, so I stood there, **Quiet As Kept**, and let Captain Riggs talk.

"Inmate Helimite, you will be held in administrative confinement pending transfer, which can take up to three weeks. At this time, I'm giving you a direct order to turn around. Place your hands behind your back to be handcuffed."

I did as instructed and asked Captain Riggs for a phone call. I needed to cancel my expected visitation for the coming weekend since a letter wouldn't reach Palm Beach County in time to inform my family that I couldn't have visitation due to this unexpected confinement. Captain Riggs advised the officer escorting me to let me use the phone once I was delivered to confinement. "Any other requests or questions, Inmate Helimite?"

"Yes, sir. To the best of your knowledge, what does a good addition to your inmate population look like, Captain Riggs?"

The captain ran his hand through his brown hair, leaned back in the swivel chair he was in and laughed while rubbing his pot belly at the same time. "Well, it doesn't look like you, apparently. Regional Inspector, Ms. Queen, **hated** your undermining tactics with security at Hardee C.I. enough to the point she *respectfully* informed our Inspector here of your capabilities to manipulate and poison the correction agenda of the Florida Department of Corrections. While you're here at Calhoun, we expect for you to behave yourself and keep your head down until you transfer."

I responded, "I will behave myself, sir, but I will never keep my head down!"

CHAPTER 9

As we turned on to Silver Beach Road and crossed the railroad tracks, the pawn shop we were about to invade was on our right, a good 30-yards away from the main road. It had a big sign in the front window that said, "We sell guns." And guns was what I needed but I wasn't buying any. Not tonight anyway.

The rain was steady pouring down and we headed to the back of the establishment to stay out of sight from any passersby. Everyone got out the cars except for Pus Head, who knew his assignment was to back his vehicle straight through the back wall and then proceed to grab bullets for the firearms that we were getting. Pus Head hit the gas and the vehicle flew backwards, crashing into the concrete wall. He created more than enough space for us to get in and out. An explosion of sound from the concrete crumbling, glass shattering, and the crunch of the debris under our feet was all I could hear.

We had scoped out this pawnshop the week before. We knew exactly where everything was and what we wanted and needed. Me and Rufus smashed display cases, acquiring top of the line handguns. Big Boy grabbed assault rifles with Spaghetti Man. And Pus Head was supposed to be grabbing ammunition, but he was nowhere to be seen. My adrenaline was running high. No alarm system went off yet and that was strange. Before I could yell out to everybody, "Hurry up. Let's go," the alarm system came to life. It created more than enough noise to get us moving up outta there.

We jumped into the two Iroc-Z Chevy's. Big Boy, Rufus, and I were in one car. Pus Head and Spaghetti Man were in the other. Big Boy spun out of there like the police was already behind us. Once we got out to Silver Beach Road, I told him, "Man, slow down and do the speed limit. Ain't nobody chasin' us."

I could see the other Iroc-Z trailing us. We took Silver Beach Road all the way to S Avenue. We did the speed limit through S Avenue and stopped at a red light at Blue Heron Boulevard. We could hear sirens and see police cars racing to where we had just hit the lick. The light changed and we passed by John F. Kennedy Junior High School, home of the Mighty Vikings.

I thought to myself, *Helimite it was just yesterday, seems like, you was in class there getting the education your parents and parent's parents fought so hard for you to have. Yet here you are throwing it all away.*

I guess Mr. Perry, security at Kennedy Junior High was right when he told me, "You gonna end up dead or in jail if you don't get it together." Our Principal, Pop King, was a different story. All he wanted to do was beat some sense into me with that paddle he carried around with him all over school campus.

The sound of another siren brought me back to the present situation. We were passing through Federal Gardens neighborhood now just two minutes away from Stoneybrook. Rufus looked over at me, "We got a lotta guns and gold."

I responded with a puzzled look on my face, "Gold?"

Rufus said, "Yeah. Pus Head was in the jewelry section getting jewelry. I saw him with my own eyes."

"Well, he gon' split that gold with all of us too," I responded.

Rufus said, "I'm sure, by now, they stashed all that jewelry in that car they're in."

"Yeah, you're probably right, Rufus," Big Boy responded. "But we gon' search that car!"

"Hell yeah," we all responded together. Then Big Boy did that crazy sounding laugh of his.

We pulled into Stoneybrook, which is one way in and one way out. We drove straight to the rear parking lot where the streetlights were out because every kid with a bb gun in Stoneybrook had shot the lights out as target practice. This was where the majority of all illegal activity went down at in Stoneybrook. There was nothing but open field behind the parking lot. The open field had different pathways that led to the back of Mangonia Park and another to West Palm Beach. From the back side of the Jai Alai on 45th Street, there were multiple ways to flee from the back of Stoneybrook if need be. More importantly, there were numerous apartments we could easily be hidden in, to avoid capture.

The rain wasn't letting up and we were all soaked as we gathered everything and went to Fat Pop's apartment. His place was always a safe haven plus his mama was never home. I knocked on the door. Fat Pop opened the door, looked at all our wet faces and bags in our hands and asked, "Y'all gonna leave me something?"

I responded, "Hell yeah. I got you, Pop, now move your big ass to the side." He had LL Cool J, *My Radio,* playing on the stereo and a porn movie on the T.V. Everybody followed me to Pop's bedroom. I started dumping my bag of guns on to the bed and everybody else did as well. There had to be at least 38 different handguns and 15 rifles, pump shotguns, 30-30, a machine gun with a pistol grip on the front and a clip as long as a twelve-inch ruler. It had M60 engraved on the side of its barrel. There was also a variety of ammunition boxes.

Fat Pop walked in his bedroom, gave us each a towel to dry off with. "Whoever y'all finna go to war with is in a world of trouble."

I looked directly at Fat Pop and told him, "You absolutely right. Hot Dog and his squad *hated* me enough to shoot up my aunt's car while I was in it at that Amoco gas station on Blue Heron, then they jumped me at the New Edition concert so they gotta *respectfully* reap what they have sown!"

CHAPTER 10

Apalachee Correctional Institution (A.C.I.) was one of the oldest prisons in the state of Florida. It opened in 1949. The only older prison than A.C.I. was Glades Correctional Institution, which opened in 1932. The events that led me to four different prisons since entering the system in 1988 was stressful and enlightening all at the same time.

Apalachee Correctional Institution is located in Sneads, Florida. It was just about 25 miles north of Calhoun C.I. in Blountstown and no more than 15-minutes away from the Georgia state line. The smell that was in the air made you want to hold your breath and not breathe at all. It wasn't stink but rather stank, which meant it was a constant smell, as it was told to me by the transport officer who had just delivered me, and this white guy named Kearns to A.C.I. The officer said, "You boys are in prime position to make a lot of money if you behave and play your cards right."

"How's that?" Kearns asked.

The officer responded in a heavy southern accent, "Well, Inmate Kearns, it's a chicken farm right there to your left over yonder, behind them row of trees there. If you stay out of trouble, which I doubt you will because you are a young and bullheaded kid, you can earn up to 20-cent an hour."

Kearns looked at the officer with a scowl on his face as he spoke, "20-cent an hour? I'm not working anybody's chicken farm for 20-cents an hour or 20-dollars an hour!"

I busted out into laughter and chimed in, "You talking my language, Kearns. As bad as them chickens smell from here, I don't want to work around them or eat any chicken as long as I'm here."

As I took in a 360 view, I could see the red brick army barracks style dormitories and all the bright orange clay soil across the landscape. This was a clear signal that I was up north and close to the Georgia state line where that bright, orange clay starts to become visible everywhere.

Kearns broke the silence with a question for the transport officer. "We should be able to get a hot breakfast still since we here this early, right?"

The officer responded, "Once I get you two over to Medical and uncuffed and unshackled, I will call the kitchen and ask them to make two regular Styrofoam trays. Neither one of you are on a special diet, right?"

Me and Kearns both answered, "No." I added, "If they're serving pork this morning, I want peanut butter for the alternate."

The transport officer said, "Okay," as he tried to find the right key to enter a side door to another red brick building. I assumed that this door had to be a side entrance into the Medical Department. We entered a white tiled hallway, and the air conditioner had to be set on freezing because me and Kearns both said at the same time, "Damn! It's cold in here." The transport officer quickly addressed us both, "Cut the profanity out. Your voices carry through these medical hallways."

Once we made it to medical intake, the chains and cuffs came off. Our temperature, weight, and pulse rate were taken and logged into our medical file. The nurse that was attending to us was around 5'8" with brown hair. She walked and had a gap between her thighs that led me to believe that she must have ridden horses her whole entire life. Kearns kept looking at me to see if I was looking at what was before us. I gave him an up-and-down nod as a signal to him that, "Hell yeah I see what this nurse is working with."

Her name was Nurse Hobbs, and she was strutting her stuff. "Where y'all coming from?" she asked.

Kearns responded, "Calhoun C.I."

"You can't be from Florida with that accent," Nurse Hobbs stated.

Kearns mouth turned up in a smirk, "No ma'am. I'm not from this lock-you-up-for-anything state. I'm from Proctorville, Ohio."

Nurse Hobbs and I said at the same time, "Proctorville, Ohio?"

I asked Kearns, "What the hell you doing way down here?"

Kearns responded, "Aw hell I was in Fort Lauderdale repairing powerlines damaged from Hurricane Gordon. I went out to a bar with a few of my co-workers and this one fat-mouth electrician kept going on and on about how us northerners were coming down south taking all the work from the local electricians."

Nurse Hobbs sipped on her cup of coffee intently listening to Kearns telling his story.

Kearns continued, "I tried to explain to this clown that we were repairing power lines and not electrical stuff inside of a house or apartment. He got pissed off and started yelling that 'it's all the same work.' I screamed back that, 'you're a dumb ass,' and I started to walk away from him, but he decides to take a swing at me, punching me in the back of the head. The force of his punch was soft as hospital cotton, so I turned around and began to connect left and right knuckles to his face. He stumbled all over the chairs and tables trying to stay upright so he wouldn't fall but me and Jack was just too much for that cock sucker."

Nurse Hobbs interrupted him, "Wait a minute. You and Jack? You and your co-worker Jack beat the guy up?"

"Nope," Kearns said with a crooked smile on his face. "It was me alone, but Jack Daniels was in my system."

The whole room erupted with laughter and Kearns continued with his story. "My co-workers were pulling me off the guy and trying to get me out of there before the cops came but it didn't work out that way. The cops were already entering the building. A cop tried to pull my arm behind my back, and I spun around and clocked his ass, knocking him out cold. By then, the damage was already done. Another cop pulls his gun out, had me lay down on the floor and put my hands behind my back. I complied and my hands have been behind my back in handcuffs, ever since, for battery on a law enforcement officer and assault for the one guy who punched me in back of my head."

All I could say was, "Damn, Kearns. You got dealt a bad hand on that."

Kearns responded, "Hell yeah."

The transport officer spoke up and added, "Well, you know the old saying in the prison system is if you keep your nose clean, you can get out on good behavior much earlier."

Kearns responded, "Well, I'm not gonna hold my breath on that ever happening. I understand where I'm at and what I'm up against in this prison system. I have a release date, but it will always be subject to change because

I'll never let anybody take my balls in here."

I responded, "Well Kearns, you talkin' my language. My thoughts exactly!"

After we finished our medical intake, they assigned us to an orientation dorm for a week. The orientation dorm was clean enough to eat off the floor without the three-second rule. Dorms like this was all for show and tell. They would have news stations come in and do interviews inside of this dorm and give the public this view of prison conditions, portraying prison life as being nice and neat and under control when the reality was the complete opposite.

Once the yard opened up and we were free to go outside, I grabbed my Super II Radio and hit the door. I had been spending so much time in confinement lately, I embraced every opportunity to go outdoors. The moment I stepped outside, the smell from that chicken farm slapped me right in my face. I had to walk about 40-yards to, what appeared to be, a small red brick and glass guard shack. As I approached the guard shack, the first thing I saw was a thick, red King James Version Bible sitting on a desk next to a phone and walkie-talkies. I moved forward to make myself visible to whoever the officer was at this security checkpoint. To my surprise, it was a light-brown skinned officer whose name tag read, "Officer Bell." Her hair was done in a finger-wave style, and she wore ruby red lipstick that sat on some of the biggest lips I had ever seen. When she spoke, her tongue was always visible as if she was smacking on some good food or something.

"Inmate, where you trying to go?"

"To the rec yard, Ms. Bell," I said her name like I been knowing her for years.

"Let me see your I.D."

I held my I.D. up against the glass so she could log my information in. When she was done, she pushed a button and the lock on the gate made a loud clicking sound. I pushed my way through it and turned my radio up to the sounds of Biggie Smalls. *I love it when you call me big papa / throw your hands in the air if you a true playa*, the song went. So, I lifted my left hand up in the air because my radio was in my right hand and went to moving my left hand from side to side because I was most definitely a true player from Palm Beach County.

As I walked toward the rec yard, the guard shack where Ms. Bell was at came to life. "Inmate Helimite, report back to center gate," the intercom system said. I turned around and popped back through the gate where

Ms. Bell stood with her hands on her hips and, what appeared to be, a whole attitude on her face.

I spoke, "Yes, ma'am?"

She responded, "I don't know where you think you're at, inmate, but this isn't a block party down in Miami so turn that music off until you're actually on the rec yard. Didn't you receive a Apalachee Correctional Institution Handbook?"

"Yes, ma'am, I did," I responded.

"Well, you need to read it before you end up getting that radio took. If one of my sergeants or captains would have heard that radio and saw you waving your arm from left to right, you would be getting some paperwork instead of counseling."

"Yes, ma'am. I understand but I have two questions to ask."

"What is it, Inmate Helimite?"

"One, if I would have been playing gospel music instead of Biggie Smalls, would you have called me back up here? And two, do you even realize how sexy you be looking when you have an attitude?"

Officer Bell tilted her head to one side, her eyes narrowed, and took a closer look at me and declared, "Oh, you trying to go to confinement today. You trying the wrong officer right now, inmate Helimite."

I responded, "Officer Bell, I have read y'all inmate handbook backward and forward and it doesn't say anywhere in that handbook where I can go to confinement for complimenting a staff member."

Officer Bell looked me up and down and said, "Keep your compliments to yourself, inmate Helimite, because flattery will get you nowhere with me but in confinement. Now, goodbye."

I turned around and mumbled to myself, "That was round one."

CHAPTER 11

April 7th, 1986. 12:00 midnight.

Me, Rufus and Big Boy were all strapped with rapid fire headed to Hot Dog's house to wait on him in a Monte Carlo that was stolen from the Palm Beach Mall earlier that night. It was a clear night in Riviera Beach, Florida and I was in deep thought about what I was about to do. Big Boy, on the other hand, could care less. He was listening to 99.1 FM, which was a Hip Hop and R&B station broadcasting out of Miami, Florida. At that moment, they were playing *Brass Monkey* by the Beastie Boys. Rufus, on the other hand, was in the back seat eating potato stix and steady telling Big Boy to turn the music down.

The more we waited, the more impatient Big Boy got. He asked, at one point, "Helimite, can't we just shoot the house up?"

"Hell naw," Rufus responded before I could. "I didn't come here to shoot up no house. The house ain't did nothing to Helimite."

He's right. The house has nothing to do with this. We're here to put Hot Dog ass to sleep.

It was apparent that God was with Hot Dog. That's why he hadn't shown up yet. He was last seen at the splash party at Gaines Park Pool that should have ended at midnight. It was 2:13 a.m. and I was struggling to stay awake. Tonight was the perfect night to put this situation to rest. The one thing Hot Dog did do, in my book, was set the standard and stage for gun play. The way he shot up my aunt's car at that Amoco gas station awhile back was something I had only seen on T.V. Hot Dog had brought reality and revenge into my world and tonight was the night that I intended to serve it right back to him. If only his short, sawed-off-shotgun-toting ass would come home tonight.

Big Boy turned the music back up again. Rufus instructed, "Big Boy, turn that music down. We supposed to be laying low. Remember? Not drawing unwanted attention to ourselves."

He responded with that crazy ass laugh that he always does and said, "You dead right, Rufus."

As soon as he turned down the radio, a Riviera Beach Police car came cruising down the street. I'm pretty sure that, by now, the car we're sitting in has been reported stolen. We slide way down in our seats and Big Boy whispered, "Helimite, if the police stop, we takin' him on a highspeed chase. Ain't no way we can get caught with these guns. The judge will skip over all them juvenile facilities and half-way houses and send our asses straight to an adult prison."

I responded, "You absolutely right. Now, be quiet."

The police car was passing right by us as another car, a black Chevy Nova, appeared on the street. It pulled right into the driveway of Hot Dog's mom's house and then there he appeared, the fearless leader of the Goodmark Park Crew, heading into his mama's house without a care in the world. All I could do was watch because the police were still on his street. They say the good Lord looks out for babies and fools, and tonight He was looking out for a damn fool! Somebody, somewhere, was praying for Hot Dog because the way this just played out couldn't be luck. When the police finally left off his street, Hot Dog was already behind closed doors, safe in his mother's house.

"Let's get outta here, Big Boy. I have a room at the Purple Rain for tonight."

"The Purple Rain?" he asked. "Where is that at?"

"The Knights Inn on 45th Street," I answered.

Rufus added, "I can tell you ain't gettin' no coochie, Big Boy. You don't even know about the Purple Rain!"

Big Boy laughed so hard, it sounded like he was having an asthma attack. We cranked up the Monte Carlo and headed in the direction of Mangonia Park to drop off Rufus. We pull up in front of his house and let him out. We exchanged hand slaps and I said, "We probably try again tomorrow."

Rufus responded, "Don't forget to come get me," and disappeared into his back yard.

Me and Big Boy drove to 45th Street, took a right and headed to the Knights Inn, also known as the 'purple rain.' It received that name because everything inside the rooms were purple and black and *Prince*, the singer, had a number one hit song still being heavily played on all the radio stations. *Purple Rain.*

I stuffed my M60 machine gun into my gym bag, so that it was not visible to anyone when I entered my room. Even at 3 a.m. there was always somebody, somewhere watching, especially at a hotel. I instructed Big Boy, "Get rid of the car before the police get behind you somewhere too far out for you to escape. I'll beep you tomorrow on what the next move gon' be."

He gave me a hand slap and said, "Okay. Who you got in that hotel room, Helimite?"

I told him, "A girl named Nunna."

He looked wide-eyed and very much interested in more details. "What's her last name?"

I responded, "Business. And her middle name is 'Your.' She went to Palm Beach Gardens High School." I laughed.

Big Boy stared back at me and gave me the middle finger and started laughing as well.

"Nunna Your Business, homeboy. Now get up outta here and be safe."

He nodded and pulled off. I entered my room, and it was ice cold inside. I fell back on the bed and sighed with a sense of tiredness. Even though I had a few different girls I was talking to, the only one available to stay with me overnight was Nicole. I believe she had her parent's thinking that she was staying overnight at her best friend Heather's house. I could hear the sink running in the bathroom and knew that Nicole had been waiting on me.

She was red bone with long black hair, and I had known her since the 5th grade. We had just reconnected in the 9th grade, and it had been on ever since. She was beautiful, smart, and her personality was amazing. More importantly, she kept me grounded, and I knew if anything had gone down tonight the way it was supposed to at Hot Dog's house, she would have been the perfect alibi to get me through whatever. But since it didn't, we were gonna chill and be nasty and make time fly by together tonight.

She came out of the bathroom wrapped in a towel. Her hair was tied up in a ponytail. When I sat up to look at her, she took her hair down and it fell down her shoulders. My body reacted immediately and the vision of her was turning me on. All I could think about was the Freddie Jackson song, *Tasty Love.*

I stood up from the bed and walked toward her. She clutched the towel like she was shy about her body. I put my hands on her hips and pulled her toward me while I kissed her on the neck. She moaned softly and we moved naturally toward the edge of the bed. She laid down, still grasping at the towel wrapped around her body. She turned me on in a way that my body couldn't deny. I continued to kiss her body while I peeled away the towel.

I licked and sucked on her right nipple while I massaged the other breast. She whispered, "Don't stop, Helimite."

I felt her nervousness disappear and the feel of her perfect red bone skin against mine had me throbbing and I was at full attention. I removed my pants while taking in the beauty of her naked body in front of me.

I rubbed my hands up her thighs and fingered her pussy. She moaned with pleasure. It was dripping wet, sticky, and I couldn't hide my excitement or tame the animal inside me. Half of me was in the mindset of New Edition and the Force MD type slow jam and the other half of me wanted to be straight Uncle Luke and the 2Live Crew. She must have recognized it on my face because she whispered to me, "Be gentle. Don't hurt me."

I wanted to feel her wetness around my dick. I slid the head in, and she moaned and grabbed my waist and pulled me into her. I lay on top of her thrusting slowly because I didn't want to nut too fast. But it was so tight and so wet, each stroke was getting me closer and closer to cumming. Then she wrapped her legs around me and I tried my best, but two more strokes was all it took, and I exploded inside of her. All the rage I had felt, since this whole thing with Hot Dog went down, disappeared in that moment and just for that moment.

I clearly had lost my way and chose the streets over all the home training my mother had instilled in me. I was way too young to die out here in these streets and I was so determined to handle the situation with Hot Dog as soon as I could. It was consuming too much of my time and thoughts.

As I think back how all this mess started. It was about a girl at Trail Skateway who was at the concession stand. She said she was waiting on Hot Dog. Not knowing that Hot Dog was an actual person, I tried to get my mack on while I thought she was waiting on her food. If it ain't one thing, it's another. My eyelids were so heavy, so it wouldn't be long now before I fell into a deep sleep. I prayed, "As I lay down to sleep, I pray to the Lord, my soul to keep. If I die before I wake, I pray to you Lord, my soul to take. In Jesus' name, Amen."

CHAPTER 12

The recreation yard wasn't huge, but it was decent enough for everything I planned to do. There were two basketball courts. One for the not-so-good players, the other one for the ballers. It was at least 80 degrees out here and the sun was beaming. I sat up high in the bleachers to watch the ballers ball. You can learn every nickname at the prison just from sitting and watching a basketball game. Cartoon. Mater Head. Lee Lee. Junkie Slim. So many different nicknames from all over the state of Florida. Incarcerated ballers running and jumping and pushing that basketball to the hoop. Being a baller myself, I could already determine who I would be a good fit with on a team.

There were a lot of inmates walking around on the rec yard as if they had no cares in the world. They appeared to be so at peace. I overheard one inmate holler, "Fat Cat! I got next on the pool table. If you wanna play, you need to bring your fat ass on."

Pool table? I say to myself. I let my eyes follow the two guys to a short flight of stairs that led to a basement. I grabbed my radio and headed in that direction. I walked down the six steps and opened the door to an indoor recreation room – four pool tables, two T.V.'s and a bathroom. Two black rec officers were inside along with a thick cloud of cigarette smoke hanging in the air. The smoke didn't seem to be circulating out of the basement. It was just still. Somebody somewhere must have read my mind because moments later a huge fan was turned on and it cleared the tobacco smoke out, to an extent.

There were at least 30 people inside the basement and just as many packs of tobacco that was clearly being used to place bets with. At one pool table was a cat named Top Secret. I knew him from Polk C.I. He was talking loud and sinking the 8-ball in the corner pocket all at the same time and adding packs of cigarettes to a laundry bag.

"The game of pool," Top Secret yelled, "isn't a fast-paced game. You city boys used to that fast-paced life. Us country boys like it slowed down. That's why we so good at shootin' pool and taking all y'all money and cigarettes. Ain't that right, P-Cola?" It was short for Pensacola, Florida.

"Hell yeah, Top Secret. That's what we do!" They gave each other a hand slap.

Top Secret called out, "P-cola, give me one of them *Newport* cigarettes you smokin' on." He lit up and inhaled the tobacco as he surveyed the room at the same time. He looked over at me and commented, "Well, I'll be damned. Look what the wind has blown our way. Helimite! When you got here?"

"I got here yesterday," I responded. "How long you been here, Top Secret?"

"Right at a year now. All I can tell you is welcome to Viet Nam, Helimite. Shit be crazy around here. Half the inmates here be high as a kite."

I responded, "Well at least they got weed on the compound."

"Weed?" Top Secret looked dumbfounded while he puffed on his cigarette. "Man, weed is hard to find up here. The white boys have they own li'l circle that goes to the visiting park on the weekend. They have their girlfriends pack their pussy then they smuggle it in by either swallowing some balloons or sticking it up they butt. We call it that doodoo reefer. It be so stank but burn good. But you never know when they gonna have it."

"Well, if it's that hard to find, how is everybody so high?"

"Helimite, they high off that *Thorazine* medication. Apalachee Correctional Institution is a psyche camp."

Now it's my turn to look dumbfounded. "Psyche camp?" I asked.

"Yeah, man. At 3:00 p.m. watch how long that medication pill line be on the side of medical. That line be long as I-95."

I'm standing there taking in all this information. I finally said, "What the hell I'm here for? I'm not crazy and yo' ass ain't either, Top Secret!"

"Helimite, they gotta have a few hundred sane people here to help run the prison. The crazies on medication can't be cooks in the kitchen or law clerks in the library, etc."

"I can dig it, bro. I haven't seen classification yet, so I don't know where I'll be assigned at for a job."

Well, good luck with that. These white folks up here strictly by the book, so don't expect no favors. But in the meantime, Helimite. How 'bout me, the Top Secret from Tampa, Florida, challenge you, Helimite from Palm Beach County, in a game of pool?"

"I don't play pool, Top Secret. I play cards. Remember? Poker or Georgia Skin. So, catch me at the card table." I picked up my radio and turned up the sound to Brandy's new song, *Best Friend*. The bass was thumpin' good on this soundtrack. I'm pretty sure this will be a let's-get-on the-dancefloor type moment in the clubs in Palm Beach County. Not a day goes by that I don't miss or have thoughts of home even with the amount of time I had ahead of me. 55 years is a lot and yet I still retain the desire to want to reach home again. It's only 1994 and my release date was 2024.

I walked out of that smoke-filled basement back into the sun and fresh air. As soon as I did, I hear someone call my name, "Helimite! Was-sup!" I looked over to my right and a skinny kid with a familiar face reached out to give a hand slap. I tried to recall where I knew him from. He finally said, "Helimite. This Reggie. Speedy li'l brother from Stoneybrook."

My mind went back in time, and I still can recall Reggie riding his new skateboard and playing with his *Tonka* truck he had got for Christmas. I asked him how Speedy was doing. He said that he was okay and that he had called and talked to him the day before. "What your young ass doing in prison, Reggie?"

He looked at me and shook his head from left to right and answered, "I was trying to come up and got popped."

If I had a dollar for every time I heard that same exact line, I'd have a pocket full of money. Reggie couldn't be no more than 17 standing here before me at a hundred-fifty pounds, wide-eyed, smoking a cigarette.

"Helimite, they don't call me Reggie no more."

"Oh yeah?" I asked. "What they call you now?"

"They nicknamed me Dirt because I get down and dirty."

I scanned over Reggie and thought to myself how a whole juvenile generation had been ushered into the Florida Department of Corrections and was being state raised. I knew Reggie's whole family. I wondered how he got out of sight from his daddy or big brother, Speedy, to end up in the prison system at 17. It was mind blowing but then again, my dumb ass had committed murder in the first degree at 17, so why am I surprised. The younger generation that watched me and maybe even looked up to me, witnessed me throw my whole life away with the crime I committed. I recognized the error of my ways now but back then it was all about money, power, and ***respect***. Through my young eyes and the young eyes watching me, the quickest way to obtain money, power and ***respect*** back then was by hustling and carrying a pistol at all times to protect and enforce your hustle.

"Reggie, I'm not calling you Dirt even though you stayed playing in the dirt in the back of Stoneybrook with your Tonka truck. You gon' always be Reggie to me."

Reggie shrugged his shoulders and nodded his head up and down and agreed. I asked, "How your fine-ass cousin Keyshia doing?"

He laughed and said that she was doing alright.

We were going back down memory lane when another young brother walked by. He was wearing a pair of *Air Jordans*, some gym shorts and a v-neck tshirt. He nodded, "Wassup, Dirt?" He gives Dirt a hand slap and a hug all at the same time.

"I'm just chillin' with my homeboy, Helimite. This my dog, Cartoon from Orlando."

We exchanged head nods of ***respect*** and Cartoon kept it moving down the hill as if he was on a mission. Cartoon couldn't be no more than 17 as well, so I asked Reggie why he didn't get sent to a youth offender prison. Reggie stated that A.C.I. had a dormitory for youth offenders but when bed space wasn't available in the youthful offender dorms, they would get pushed into general population with adult prisoners.

I was pretty sure that particular procedure was against the law especially if the youth offender was not tried and convicted as an adult, but this was 1994 and prison overcrowding was at an all-time high. The Department of Corrections was filling up beds and being paid for every bed that it filled. The prison system was all about the almighty dollar and it was finding more and more ways to make money off inmate labor. It was modern day slavery coming into full view.

I had been at Apalachee just two days and found out that half the inmates here were on a prescription drug called *Thorazine*. A quarter were juveniles, and the last quarter were grown men and supposedly all in their right mind, at least enough to assist in the day-to-day operations of the prison. I can see why Top Secret said, "Welcome to Viet Nam." With the combination of the Florida sun, juveniles, people on crazy medication, the stank from the chicken farm and no weed to be smoked – this was a riot waiting to happen.

"Attention on the compound. The yard is now closed. All inmates report to your dormitory immediately."

CHAPTER 13

As I made my way back to my dorm, Kearns walked up beside me. He was sweating like he had been playing ball. "Kearns, what the hell you been doing?" I asked.

"Playing handball. That's part of my workout. It keeps my wind up and my arms loose and limber," he responded. "And I jogged two miles."

"Two miles?" I repeated. "If your ass having any thought of trying to escape, you need to be jogging at least ten miles a day because them dogs and helicopters gon' be trackin' yo' ass down."

Kearns looked at me sideways and said, "Escape? That's the furthest thing from my mind, Helimite."

"That's what all them white boys say in the beginning, Kearns. Did you leave a girlfriend behind, back in Kentucky?"

He quickly corrected me, "Ohio, Helimite."

I laughed, "Yeah. Ohio."

"Yeah, I have a girl back home."

"Y'all still on good terms?" I asked.

He said, "Kinda."

"What you mean, kinda? You either are or not. There's no in between, Kearns!"

He rubbed his chin and answered, "I agree but I'm not asking for any relationship advice. I'm just trying to get to the shower before they start count."

"I know what you mean, Kearns. The officers can do the math when it comes to the money amount on their check stubs, but they catch hell trying to count how many inmates are here for every count time."

As we continued to our dorm, two sergeants were posted up on the sidewalk watching the movements of everyone heading back to their dorm. One sergeant is white, at least 6'10" and looks like a tight end for an NFL team. The other sergeant is black, around six-feet tall and built like Mike Tyson. The only difference is his arms. They are three times bigger than Mike Tyson and as I got closer to him, it was plain to see that this sergeant was cross-eyed. He could be looking right but his eyeballs were watching everything left.

"What the fuck you looking at, inmate?" He screamed at somebody in front of me. "Get your shirt tucked in and get your punk ass to your dorm," he shouted.

The inmate threw his hands in the air and said, "Damn, Sarge, you ain't got to talk to me like that. My mama ain't raise no punk."

Sarge, with his deep voice and slow drawl said, "If you don't like what I just said, inmate, I got a understanding room I can take you to, mutha-fucka. Now pull them goddamned pants up some more."

The white sergeant was Sheely and the black sergeant was named Dunlap. I would find out through conversations with Reggie a.k.a. Dirt, that these two sergeants were the main headbangers at the prison and they were also part of the goon squad at the prison. The goon squad handled all the ma-jor search details and all the suppose-to-be inmates that thought they were gorillas. They received the nickname goon squad from the inmate popula-tion, but their Department of Corrections title was Special Response Team.

Me and Kearns eased our way past the two sergeants without inci-dent. As soon as I entered the dorm, I took a piss and sat down on my bunk. I sat there processing all the info I had gathered today when the dorm P.A. sys-tem came to life. "Mail call! Mail call! All inmates, listen up for your name." My name was the eighth name they called, and I was curious and excited to see who had taken the time out of their busy life to drop me a few lines. I hadn't been at A.C.I. long enough to send all my loved ones and friends my new address, so I knew that whatever mail I had was mail that was addressed to Hardee C.I. or Calhoun C.I. and had been forwarded here to A.C.I.

I walked up to the officer's station window and showed my I.D. The officer handed me three pieces of mail and an Ebony magazine. As I sifted through the mail to see who all had written to me, I see the most important female name in my life – Dorothy Mae Jones. I broke the seal of tape on the letter in a hurry and began to read.

> *Hello Son. I'm sure all is well for you and with you because the prayers of the righteous availeth much and you, my son, are always and forever in my prayers. I mapped out the trip to visit you. It's about five hours but to God be the glory. He is good and he makes ways out of no ways. Grace and peace be multiplied to you from Jesus Christ, our Lord and Savior and soon coming king. Son, always remember to read the Bible for encouragement and enlightenment. God is always thinking of you. He has kept you safe this far through a whole lot of trouble. He will never leave you or forsake you. The Lord is my helper and my strength and he is and will continue to provide. God is faithful always.*
>
> *We had a revival last week, son, and a guest speaker who is a prophet of God asked if there was anyone here with a son in prison and I answered, "Yes!" And he told me God was about to do a miracle for you and you are coming home soon! So, continue to hold on by faith and not by sight in Jesus' name. Your sisters and brothers are all well. The nieces and nephews. Also, your grandmother asked about you so you know what that means. Call or write her son. We love you. Read your Bible. Book of Psalms.*
>
> *Love You Much,*
> *Mom*

I read the letter twice and a sense of calmness settled over me. There's nothing like hearing from my mama. It's like hearing from her and being in church all at the same time. I miss going to church. The prisons have a chapel but it's all surface stuff. You have to hope and wait for the right outside church to come in to bring the word of God and pray with you and over you. A lot of prisoners looked down on and frowned upon the inmates who go to church or the chapel. They seemed to think it was a sign of weakness, for whatever reason, but I know better because of my upbringing, and I have read the Bible. There's a lot of knowledge in that book to be absorbed if you open your heart and mind to what's being said. I'm no saint, by far, but I know what God has brought me and my family through. Gangsters, crooks, pimps, and players all pray to God, sooner or later, for help and guidance pertaining to some unforeseen event or crisis that's bigger than them. Trust me. I know. I am a living testimony.

I gotta call mama before the weekend to notify her that I have been moved, so that five-hour trip she mapped out might be nine or ten hours now. She is not gonna like that, but I have no control over where these white folks decide to transfer me to.

I looked down at the last two letters I had received. One was from Octavia and the other from Ritha. I read them both, gazed at the pictures Ritha sent, then added them to my photo album.

The officers finally announced count time. I sat up in the upright position and sighed, hoping this count didn't drag out. After 30 minutes, the dorm officer finally announced, "Clear," and the race was on as inmates ran to the telephone and showers before it all cuts off at 10 p.m.

I grabbed my Dove soap and headed to the shower with all kinds of thoughts and stuff on my mind. Because I chose to take my time getting to the shower, all the hot water was gone, so I didn't stay in there as long as I normally would. I dried off, put my boxer shorts and t-shirt on, and stopped to look at the bulletin board where the next day's callout sheet was. To my surprise, I had two callouts. One with Mental Health at 8:30 a.m. And the other with Classification at 10:00 a.m. Further up the bulletin board was the Department of Corrections menu and tomorrow's breakfast was French toast with a sausage patty and oatmeal. I looked to my left and the phone line was extremely long, so I decided to pay one of these cats whose bunk was close to the phone to get the phone for me tomorrow night, as soon as 8:00 count clears. A soup or honey bun will go a long way in prison when inmates be broke and have no hustle or support from home.

I got back to my bunk, put on some deodorant, and sprinkled some baby powder inside my t-shirt to help me stay cool and dry. The dormitory was so hot even with the ceiling fan on. Nothing but hot air was being circulated. I grabbed my radio and found a smooth groves radio station my homeboy Reggie, a.k.a Dirt, had told me about. I plugged in my headphones and George Benson's song *Give Me the Night* was coming through crystal clear, no interference from other FM stations. I propped my pillow up and laid back to watch the movement within the dorm.

I thought about writing Octavia and Ritha but it would be lights out here soon, so I just lay there, tried to relax and sort out my thoughts and plans, as if I had other options. Aaron Hall's song, *I Miss You*, came on. I do all I can to try not to reminisce about past loves of my life.

It's 1994, and other than my mama and siblings, don't nobody love me no more. I've been gone eight years and still have a boat load of time to do in front of me. It would be nice to lay eyes on Beth or Nicole. Beth was dating Leon, or was it PeDo, last I heard. And Nicole was in college in Louisiana now. Everybody had a life to live, so I get it. I'll have to just cherish the memories I had with them to move me past these moments. The last song I remember hearing was Teddy Pendergrass, *Love TKO*, before I drifted off to sleep.

CHAPTER 14

I woke up at 4 a.m. because I could no longer hold the urine in my bladder. I'm surprised at how many people are up and moving around at four in the morning. The midnight shift was in the building and a nice looking, blonde-haired white girl was in the officer's station standing up, playing with her hair. Her all-male audience were watching her every move. Guys were in the shadows everywhere, getting their lust on. I approached the bathroom, walked up to the urinal, relieved myself, and made a b-line back to my bunk. I tuned my radio to a hip hop station, put my headphones back on and listened to Warren G rap about *Regulators*. I could smell a Black and Mild cigar in the air. It smelled good even though I didn't smoke. It was still hot as hell in this dorm even in the middle of the night. It wasn't too long before all the lights came on in the dorm, which was the alarm clock to get yourself up if you're going to eat breakfast.

I raised up, grabbed my washcloth, toothbrush, and toothpaste and headed back to the bathroom to kill whatever dragon breath I had created overnight. I took a deep breath, shook my head, and said to myself, *another day among the living behind the razor wire*. 15 minutes later, the dorm officer released our dorm for breakfast and all 90 of us lined up for the short walk over to the chow hall. One of the first things you learn about prison pretty fast is that you line up single file for every damn thing, and my scary ass always stayed at the back of the line so I could watch everything in front of me.

I noticed Kearns was always in the back with me. Looks like me and Kearns had an unspoken bond with each other. No matter where you're at, real always recognize real. I was always taught to treat everybody with **respect** until they showed you that they're not deserving of your **respect**. I stuck to that code regardless of whatever crime anybody had committed. We were all in here together until we E.O.S., expiration of sentence or die. And dying was the furthest thing from my mind. I had too much to live for.

After 20 minutes of waiting in line, I finally received a tray with two pieces of French toast, sausage, and oatmeal. The syrup was so watered down I didn't even use it. As I finished eating, I thought about my classification call out at ten and I silently hoped they didn't assign me to this kitchen because of my cooking experience back at Polk C.I. But, first things first. I had to report to Mental Health at eight. What they wanted with me, I didn't know, but I would find out here shortly. The sun hadn't risen to its full potential yet. There was just a hint of light beginning to crack the sky as we walked back to our dorm and back to our bunks to be counted once again for the next shift coming on.

It seemed like every prison I've been to since I left Polk C.I. had been crazy. Polk C.I. had an older crowd of convicts that set the tone and pace for just about everything. Yeah, good ole Polk C.I. It seemed crazy to sit here and actually say that I missed an actual prison, but you had to be there and be in the loop to really understand the vibe there.

I laughed to myself as I thought about the time me, Ant, Rufus, and Freddie Jay were all headed to the laundry room to pick up our clean clothes for the week and when the laundry worker handed us our bags, Ant's bag was new and all the clothes in his bags were pressed and folded. So, Rufus asked Ant, "Who you paying in this laundry to press and fold your clothes?"

Ant shrugged his shoulders and said, "Shit. Nobody."

I responded, "Ain't no way they doing all that for free. Look at our clothes in our bags, Ant." I opened my bag to show Ant the crumpled mess happening in my laundry bag.

Ant was looking awkward now as he motioned to the laundry worker to come back. Ant questioned him, "Hey man, who back there pressing and folding my clothes like this?"

The laundry worker asked to look at his laundry bag and pointed to a red dot on Ant's bag and said, "Dee Dee is doing your laundry bag."

All four of us holler, "Dee Dee," at the same damn time.

Ant's face went flat with disbelief. He rebounded quickly though and slammed his palm down on the laundry counter. "I don't know who the fuck Dee Dee is but tell him come here."

The laundry worker disappeared into the back where the washers and dryers were. Minutes later, this grown ass man who was trying his best to look like a girl, came out. Lip gloss on, his shirt tied in a knot in the front with his navel showing, with skin-tight pants on.

Freddie J was the first to speak, "Hell naw! Ant, I can't wait to tell my sister Diane about this." Diane was Ant's ex-girlfriend.

Rufus looked from left to right and said, "What the fuck?"

Ant wasted no time getting to the business. "Yo, listen here man," Ant said loud and clear.

Dee Dee cut him off, "I gave up on being a man a long time ago, honey. I have sucked and took way too many dicks up my ass not to be addressed as a bitch."

Ant responded, "Fuck boy, whatever you do with your mouth and ass is your business. Keep all that gay mess to yourself. I'm gonna tell you this one time only. If I come back through here again and my bag look like this, I'm gonna catch some more time for sticking some iron through you." Ant balled up his bag, threw it down on the dirt outside the door, and stomped on it.

Dee Dee stood there and watched while smacking on some chewing gum and responded, "Chile, it ain't that serious for me. I won't touch your bag again." And Dee Dee spun around and twisted his way back to the workstation.

I was laughing and trying to calm Ant down. I said, "Ant. Listen, bro. You can't get mad at Dee Dee because he's attracted to you. He was trying to show you some love."

Ant screamed, "Stop playing with me, Helimite! I'm not with that shit. I will send that punk home in a box, dog. I ain't the one."

"Well, dog, you need to stop all that working out. You done got fine and you bowlegged, and it looks like all the women and punks are all sweatin' you now, Ant."

"Once again, stop playin' with me, Helimite," Ant responded, irritated, while all the rest of us continued to laugh.

CHAPTER 15

"Count is clear," the P.A. system echoed through the dorm. "Work call! Work call!" the officer announced. "All inmates report to your assigned jobs, immediately."

I jumped off my bunk and reached into my locker and grabbed my eye drop bottle. I twisted the cap off and squeezed two drops of Safari cologne by Ralph Lauren into my hand, rubbed them together, and hit my neck and arms with it. Ain't no way I'm going to the Mental Health building smelling like every other prisoner here. I had to get some separation, which was always important in prison. We all wore the same prison clothes, same color, but my shoe game, jewelry, cologne, and of course my conversation and demeanor kept me in a different light with staff, no matter where I went.

I secured my radio in my locker and hit the door. I saw Kearns bouncing a handball, headed to the rec yard. I called out to him, "I'll be out there in a few to see if you really know how to play handball, Kearns."

He laughed, "Anytime you ready, Helimite."

I nodded and kept it moving. I arrived at the Medical Building where the Mental Health Department had a few offices that they operate out of. I showed the medical officer my I.D. He looked at his clipboard and checked my name off his callout sheet.

He told me to have a seat and absolutely no talking.

I mumbled, "Shit, the first amendment is the freedom of speech but in prison you lose all your rights, pretty much." I sat down, looked at my Scottie Pippen Flight edition Nikes on my feet and reached down to string up my right shoelace. It's too cold inside this medical lobby. There were fake plants spread out to try and give the place a homely feel, I guess. But the walls were overdue for some fresh brown and beige paint. The last layer they had added was peeling badly.

I heard some heels clicking and clacking against the tile floor. Somewhere down the hall, the sound of it was getting louder as they approached the lobby. The woman had a file in her hand and called out, "Inmate Helimite."

I looked in her direction and said, "Yes ma'am."

She responded, "Follow me, please."

"Absolutely." I am so taken with her flawless beauty and the way she moved in her high heel shoes. She looked just like the soul sister, Pam Grier in them Black 70's movies, afro and all. She stood about 5'8", light brown skin, and sexy as hell. She wore a cream-colored pantsuit with a black belt and black heels. The sister was fine. All I could do was walk behind her and admire the curves.

She came to a stop at an office with the name 'Doctor White,' written on the door. I took a deep breath and exhaled because I knew this super fly secretary was now handing me off to Doctor White. She entered the office and went behind a huge desk with all kinds of paperwork neatly arranged on her desk, along with four Department of Corrections mental health files. I could plainly see my prison number, 182456 on the very top file. It was thin compared to the other three files because I had never sought help for mental issues. To my knowledge, I had none. I handled all my problems through prayer, smoking weed, lifting weights and calling my mama. So, why was I here? I had no clue.

Dr. White began to speak. I listened to her every word while my eyes scanned her office. There were plaques and awards from the University of Texas. A picture of a little girl that couldn't be no more than eight years old. The writing on the picture frame read, "I love me some Ki."

Dr. White must have noticed that she didn't have my full attention because she called my name. "Helimite! Are you through inventorying my office?"

"Yes, ma'am. It's not every day that I meet someone of your caliber."

"I appreciate the kind words, but I need you to focus and listen to me right now. The reason you're here is because you spent over 30 days in Calhoun Correctional Institution's confinement. You spent exactly 48 days back there, and it's not documented where anyone from Mental Health came to interview you, face to face, as required by the Department of Corrections."

I nodded my head up and down, acknowledging everything she explained. She continued, "Everything you tell me here is confidential with the exception of you telling me that you're going to hurt yourself or anyone else. Anything of that nature, I will have to report to security immediately. Do you understand?"

I responded, "Yes, ma'am."

Without hesitation, Dr. White jumped right into 21 questions.

"How did you pass the time, Helimite?"

"A lot of different ways."

She impatiently said, "I'm sure you did but can you elaborate?"

"I can and I will if you promise to stop using all those big words during our session."

She blinked those beautiful eyes a few times and laughed. "What big word did I use that sidetracked you, Helimite?"

Before she could finish her question, I said, "Elaborate."

She opened her mouth to speak but no words came out. She hiccupped. She quickly apologized and said, "These hiccups are driving me crazy." She reached for a cup with some liquid in it and swallowed. She then sat her drink down on her desk and looked at me as I sat there with my hands in my lap, trying to look as humble and innocent as I possibly could. "Now, where were we?" she asked then looked at her notes and continued, "Some inmates exercise, play out old memories, etcetera."

"I'm big on exercise. And I played out old memories so much back there that they were no longer old, but brand new to me again."

Dr. White wrote down something then asked, "So, did you have a routine? If so, what did that look like?"

"The routine I used was that I'd stay up all night so I could sleep all day. The 8 to 4 shift was something truly special at Calhoun C.I. What was so special about that shift…" I leaned back as I gathered my thoughts and continued, "Point blank, they were racist, and they did everything they could to make your stay in their confinement much longer by writing you disciplinary reports for just about anything. So, I stayed sleep or played sleep to avoid all that."

"Sounds like you had a plan, Helimite," Dr. White responded.

"Well, the more disciplinary reports you receive, the longer your stay is in the prison system, as well. So, I was thinking about my future release date even though that's many years away."

She wrote some more things on her notepad, and as she began to speak again, a hiccup came out again. She said, "Excuse me," and drank from her cup again. "Due to this bout of hiccups I'm having, Helimite, I'm going to reschedule this interview 'til next week. Are you okay with that?"

"Yes. No problem, Dr. White." Man, this woman was absolutely gorgeous. If I had to draw with pencil and paper what gorgeous was, I would draw her. Her shape and curves were breathtaking. I wondered if she knew I was lusting my ass off and was memorizing her every move to carry over with me tonight in the shower. *Calm down, Helimite, and stay in the cage, tiger,* that voice in my head said. I laughed out loud before I actually knew it.

"Helimite, are you laughing at me?"

"Of course not, Dr. White. I was laughing at something I recalled watching on In Living Color."

"Oh my God, I love that show. Especially the Homey the Clown skits."

"Yes, me too, Dr. White."

She stood up and walked from behind her desk to escort me back up front to the lobby. I was so glad I was behind her, so she couldn't see the erection I had grown in her presence.

I left that building and headed to the Classification Department for my next callout. I had to be on point up in there because I did not want a job assignment inside grounds, pushing a lawnmower or sweeping sidewalks. I needed a job inside a building, around some women.

That was the blueprint, my main man Benny Stephens a.k.a. Gigolo had given me from the very beginning at Polk C.I. in 1988. Man, how I missed Gigolo. That brother had a way of making everything seem reachable and simple to attain. And anytime I would give him his props and say, "You know, Gigolo, you dead right, my brother." His response would always be, "Of course I'm right, Helimite. I'm a gigolo. Remember?" He was my ever-resourceful pool of knowledge and direction for situations I would encounter pertaining to women. Gigolo convinced me that if she worked inside the prison, she was attainable. You just had to come up with the right approach, the right words and sometimes cash money to get her attention.

I entered the Classification Department and handed the orderly my pass to be there. He disappeared to the back. A minute or two later he reappeared and said, "Follow me." This building was old and smelled like mildew and coffee. It was all red brick just like the rest of the prison. I arrived at Mr. Ghostlon's door and was advised to have a seat. He already had my prison file open and was reading intently as he quickly turned to the next page of some report. I'm sure he was reading about me. Once he finished, he closed my file and looked up at me and said, "Inmate Helimite, welcome to Apalachee Correctional Institution."

I could already tell this wasn't going to be good. The smirk that was on his face and the tone of voice he was using had my antennas way up. He was then interrupted by a phone call. I sat there and took notice of family pictures and, what looked like, him milking a cow with a young girl who was probably his daughter. He had a sign that hung on the wall that said, "Security isn't convenient."

He ended his phone conversation and stared at me. "Inmate Helimite, I read that you have a strong way of manipulating people to do things that they should not be doing. It has been noted and highlighted in your file. We here at A.C.I. have dealt with your kind before, and I have the perfect job assignment for you."

"And what would that be, Mr. Ghostlon."

"I'm assigning you to the general warehouse. It's located in our industrial yard, next to the laundry."

I stood up to leave and Mr. Ghostlon was offended at my gesture. "Sit back down, Inmate Helimite. I wasn't finished and you don't run or dictate horse shit here at A.C.I. And if I see your name come across my desk pertaining to any illegal activities, I will bury you in our confinement. You are now dismissed, jackass."

I stood up and left his office in a hurry before the other side of me could react and say something I couldn't take back. I been spending way too much time in confinement lately. Being in open population was like being on the street. I could make moves and turn a few corners.

Once I was back outside, the stench from the chicken farm was almost suffocating. There was nothing you could do to get away from the smell. I headed to the rec yard since all my mandatory callouts had been met. I made my way to the bleachers on the softball field and sat back to watch the movement on the yard.

I'm 24 years old and really couldn't see my way out of this prison system. Maybe I needed to start hanging with the white boys, who were always scheming on a way out of here. But, even if I did escape, where would I go? What would I do? It cost money to be on the run, and I clearly don't have it like that. Man, I wish I had a joint of some good ass weed right now. Starting over at a new prison is always challenging especially when you are trying to scheme up ways to make money. At the rate I was going, it doesn't look like I'll be getting transferred anywhere close to a prison in South Florida. Some of the stories I had heard are really unbelievable, but I know everyone I talk to can't be lying about Glades Correctional Institution in Palm Beach County, a.k.a. the muck where they don't give a fuck.

Yeah, the big picture is always to go home but 2024 wasn't right around the corner, and I felt like I needed to be as comfortable as possible while I'm in this cage. The voice in my head thought – *Helimite, why on God's green earth would you want to be comfortable in prison? Uncomfortable would push you toward getting out sooner.*

Since I'm sitting all by myself, I responded out loud, "I have 55 years to do in the flesh, not in the spirit. So, fall back and watch me figure some stuff out."

"Inmate Helimite," the intercom sounds off. "Report back to your dormitory, immediately."

All I could do was shake my head and said, "Here we go again."

Helimite behind the razor wire (1994)

59

CHAPTER 16

I walked toward the center gate, showed my ID to the officer there, and the gate opened for me to proceed to my dorm. When I arrived, I saw Kearns packing all his property. I asked him, "Kearns, wassup?"

"They moving us to another dormitory. This is only a orientation dorm."

"What dorm you going to?" I asked.

"H dorm," Kearns said.

I approached the officer's station and showed my I.D. The officer grabbed a clipboard, looked at it and told me, "Pack all your shit. You're moving to G dorm, bunk 108."

"Yes, sir," I responded and turned around to pack up my personal items.

Kearns was already leaving out the door. I gathered up all my belongings and walked the short distance over to G dorm. I checked in at the officer's station. The dorm was pretty much empty right now because it was still working hours. G dorm was an open bay dorm with around 140 bunk beds. It smelled like somebody had been mopping with a sour mop head up in here. This dorm was definitely a downgrade from the orientation dorm. You could literally eat off the floor in the orientation dorm. It was so clean. The wax on the floor was so thick, it was nicknamed the Glass House.

I sat my property on my bunk and went to the bathroom. What I saw there was crazy. There were eight steel toilets, side by side, no more than four inches apart, and six urinals directly across from them. A small fan in the back was set up as an exhaust system to pull all the funk outside when it all went down. The steel toilets were so close together, there was no way you could wipe your behind without brushing up against the person sitting on the toilet to the left or right of you. No kind of privacy, period. But that is the main luxury you lose once you enter the prison system. The shower area was small as well. Six shower heads for 140 people. A sign hung over the showers, "Monday through Friday 5 a.m. – 9:30 p.m. Saturday & Sunday 7 a.m. – 9:30 p.m. The cutoff time was 9:30 p.m. because 10 p.m. was master roster count. That's when every prisoner had to give his full name and prison ID number, the number you can't or won't ever forget.

I headed back to my bunk, sat down, and breathed in deeply and then exhaled. I went from sugar to shit real fast. From a prison standpoint, this was an old ass, open bay dorm. Everything was old and out in the open to be seen by security and the inmates you were being housed with. I needed to find a way to get into a two-man room – the kind I had seen on the other side of the compound. In the meantime, I had to play the hand I was dealt – a job in the general warehouse, and this dirty ass, overcrowded open bay dorm.

At 4 p.m., the rec yard closed and all inmates had been released from their daily job duties to report back to their assigned dorms for the evening count. I lay back on my bunk to see what kind of characters I would be living in here with. They were loud and rowdy and couldn't wait to eat dinner.

"What's for chow tonight? Anybody wanna sell they chicken? I got two soups for a chicken," I heard this one heavy set brother scream out.

Somebody responded, "I call that, Fat Cat!"

Fried chicken a.k.a. barnyard pimp was like having a steak dinner in the prison system. With A.C.I. having that chicken farm, I wondered how many days a week they served chicken. My thoughts were interrupted when this midget walked up to me and said, "Hey man, you from Palm Beach?"

I looked at the midget and asked, "Yes. Why?"

He responded, "I am too. I'm Mater Head."

"I'm Helimite from Stoneybrook," I answered.

He stared at me and casually said, "I heard about you and your case back before I left the Palm Beach County Jail. I'm from downtown West Palm Beach."

I nodded my head up and down as I listened to the dorm intercom come to life, "All inmates, report to your assigned bunk for count time." I was glad to hear that announcement because it seemed like Mater Head was ready to tell me his life story, and I really just wanted to fall back and sort out all my thoughts and feelings about my current situation. I sat up in an upright position as the first C.O., correction officer, came through smoking a Black and Mild cigar. The cigar made the musky-smelling dorm smell better. I watched the old, struggling ceiling fans squeak away, trying to keep the dorm cool, but it was only circulating dry heat and Black and Mild smoke. It took about 20 minutes before they cleared count and announced for G dorm to line up for chowtime.

I figured this would be the best time and opportunity to burn off some stress by skipping chow and going straight to the recreation yard to the weight cage to work out. Of course, it would be wide open because nobody ever missed a fried chicken tray. I get in the back of the line. Once they busted the door open, there was a breezeway you had to walk down to get to the kitchen and chow hall. The breezeway was a sidewalk with a roof covering and iron railing on both sides. If it rained or snowed, yes, I did say snow, you wouldn't get wet. The breezeway also separated E and F dorm from G and H. I made a right, going down the hill to the rec yard while the rest of the dorm went left toward the kitchen to eat. At least that's what I thought.

As I got to the bottom of the hill, I walked past the dip bar and pullup bar and into the weight cage. There was one brother already in there grabbing and moving weights and benches to one corner section in the back of the weight cage. He was so focused with the dumbbells he was gathering, he didn't even notice me standing at the entrance of the cage.

I broke the silence and commented, "You gon' be big as fuck if you planning on lifting all them weights, jit."

He looked over at me and responded, "Jit? I'm getting everything I need to work with before it gets crowded in here."

I began to walk around the cage to find what I needed and no matter what I needed, he already had it. "Jit, if you not going to use that curl bar right now, let me get a few sets in with it 'til you ready for it."

He responded, "I'm Cartoon, not Jit. When the courts in Orange County decided to take me to trial as an adult and not a youth offender, the jit you think you see died in that courtroom."

I was a little shocked at his response. We both shared the same experience with being upgraded to adult status as juveniles and sent to an adult prison. But, hey, you commit serious crimes, you get serious housing.

I commented, "Cartoon. You Dirt partner, right?"

He nodded his head up and down and said, "Yeah, that's my li'l dog from Palm Beach."

"You from Orlando. I just left a bunch of your homeboys at Hardee C.I. You know Brent Abrams, Stan O, Mike Bell, and Hobo?" I asked.

"I heard those names before but the two I know is Mike Bell who is a living legend in the martial arts world in Orlando. And Brent Abrams."

I nodded. "Mike Bell was my roommate for a while and me and Brent used to smoke that trees together a lot and play basketball, third yard, after the sun had gone down."

Cartoon's eyes seemed to light up when I said that, and I noticed him starting to really look me over as if he was sizing me up for a future fight or something. Cartoon was no more than 185 pounds and maybe 6'1". Yeah, I was sizing him up as well.

"I heard it was a real bad riot at Hardee C.I. a while ago. Were you there for that riot?" I asked.

"Nope, I had already transferred. That riot was Fort Lauderdale and Orlando bumping heads about something. From what I heard, it was a lot of knife play in it so the helicopter had to be flown in to get a few of them dudes to a outside hospital. Blood was all over the recreation yard. I wonder if Hardee C.I. is still on lockdown for that one."

I shook my head from side to side at the thought of all the tension, shakedowns, and drama playing out over there. "Cartoon, you already know. Every day behind this fence isn't the same, so it's important to me to stay ready for whatever. Now, let me get that curl bar 'til you ready for it."

"Get yo' sets in, bro. I'm bench pressing first."

He put 225 on the bar and started his routine. I planned on doing curls and a set of pullups today. Tomorrow I would do a lower body workout. Cartoon had his radio playing and Brandy was singing about how she *Wanna Be Down*. I heard the steel plates being moved around. I looked over to my left and Cartoon was adding more weight to the bar. 315 was on the bar now. I said, "Cartoon, I didn't know you like fat girls. That 315 is a big bitch."

He laughed and said, "I like pussy, Helimite, and I been fuckin' this bitch for a while now."

He lay back on the bench, took a few deep breaths and lifted the weight off the rack and pushed the 315 pounds, four times and set it back on the rack. I know a challenge when I see one and this young brother had just set the stage for it.

Cartoon looked at me and said, "You in the 300 club, Helimite?"

"Last time I checked, Cartoon, I've been a member since 1988." I walked over to the bench, lay down, and got my breathing settled. I kissed the bar and said, "My steel," as I always did since 1988. I took the weight off the rack and lay it on my chest for three seconds and pushed it off me, no sweat. I repeated the same process up to five reps and sat the weight back on the rack. Me doing five instead of the four Cartoon did was my way of telling him, "I'm one up on ya." I stood up and started back to my own routine. The recreation yard was starting to get active with more people.

I left out of the weight cage and walked toward the softball outfield to do some jumping jacks and toe touches. It wasn't long before inmates were everywhere on the yard. A group of white inmates were sitting in the field playing a board game of Dungeon and Dragons. As I got closer to where they were, I could smell the weed they were smoking, trying to be discreet. I got within three feet of them and asked, "Any of that weed for sale?"

All five of them looked at me like, negro be for real, and stated, "Naw. We bought a dime sack from some Spanish guy."

I said, "Okay," and kept it moving, making a mental note of their faces.

An hour later, I noticed all the outside lights on the dormitory come on, which was a clear indication that count time was near. After taking ten steps or so, the compound PA system sounded that the yard was closed. "All inmates report to your assigned dorms for count. Count time. Count time."

CHAPTER 17

It had been four weeks since I arrived here at A.C.I. and it was hard on the yard. I had started my new job in the general warehouse and was working for Mr. Sneads. He was an older white officer whose family founded the town where this prison was built. Sneads, Florida. It didn't take long to figure out that Mr. Snead had a lot of influence at the prison. When he talked, all the staff listened. Even his superior officers followed his lead when he was present.

This general warehouse job mainly consisted of loading and unloading semi-trucks that brought food, soap, toilet paper and whatever supplies that were needed to keep a prison running. Mr. Sneads and two other officers that were assigned to the general warehouse thoroughly searched everything that entered the prison. If televisions came in, they would take the TV apart to make sure nothing illegal was hidden on the inside. You had to be really creative to get something past Mr. Sneads in Sneads, Florida.

It clearly appeared to me that the Classification Department had done its best job to isolate me from the movement of all female staff. All I could see for scenery was the laundry room 40 yards away, an old red brick smokestack and a sliver of the Chattahoochee River. If you cross over that river, you were officially in Georgia. "This too shall pass," my mama always used to say. "Just keep waking up, son, and give God the glory." I was so bored working in this warehouse. I had to come up with something to change my situation and scenery.

I had been seeing Dr. White twice a week. We had a whole lot in common. We both came from God-fearing households, loved old school R&B, and gospel. In one session, I brought several photos of me back in Riviera Beach, Florida a.k.a. "the woods," but it had grown into something so raw; they nicknamed it DA RAW. She laughed so hard at my yellow canvas *Converse* tennis shoes black *O.P.* shorts, yellow fake silk V-neck shirt and black and yellow tarpon hat. The tarpon hats were extremely popular back in the 1980's. There were so many colors they came in that you could mix it up how you wanted to and still keep them guessing.

"I bet you had some of that original green and gold bottle *Polo* cologne."

"No, ma'am, Ms. White. I was wearing that *Drakkar Noir* back then."

"My brother used to wear that. I know that smell anywhere." She blinked her eyes a few times and looked toward the ceiling as if she were trying to gather a memory. "Boy, those were the days."

I looked her dead in her eyes and stated, "Who you calling a boy? Nothing but a grown ass man right here."

"Chileeeee, you can make your mouth say anything."

"Well hear me and hear me well and understand me and understand me clear. If you not gonna give me a shot at the title, just be **quiet**," I said.

"What title, Helimite? The title to my heart? Chileee, y'all convicts are something else. You not gonna have me in the unemployment line tired, broke, and hungry." She laughed to herself like I wasn't present.

"Listen, Dr. White. I have a boat load of time left to do. This, you already know. I'm not interested in causing you any harm or pain in any way, shape or form. I'm a man no matter where I'm at. If I was to have any kind of dealing with you off the record, I would always protect your best interest because that's who I am."

"Chileeee, I have way too much to lose to even consider fooling around with you."

"Well, Dr. White, I wouldn't even pursue you if you didn't have nothing to lose. My standards are high, regardless of it all. Nothing from nothing leaves absolutely nothing. That's why I stay prayed up and keep my head to the sky. I won't be in prison forever. But there's no rush. Let's continue getting to know each other without you evaluating every topic we discuss as Dr. White, but as Linda, a mother of two from Houston, Texas."

"I can try, Helimite, but I can't make any promises on or about anything. The minute your behind starts to get caught up, disrespectful or sloppy, I will no longer be calling you out for therapy twice a week. Do you understand?"

"Of course, I do, Linda. I mean, Dr. White."

"Don't play with me, Helimite. This is how me and my kids eat."

"No problem. Relax."

She looked at me for a while, in silence, then she switched on the radio and the jam *I Like* by Guy was playing. This was the indication that my session was now over for today.

CHAPTER 18

Time was waiting for no one. It was moving right along. It was football season, and the weeks were flying by. I still hadn't found a way to get any weed in and I was determined not to buy the crumbs the white boys were trying to sell on the low, every now and then. This was the furthest I had ever been from home and even though I was far away, I was hoping my mama would come visit me on Christmas as she always did.

I was all over the place in my thoughts. I was on my bunk looking through old pictures in my photo album. I was just wondering and curious about how all my family and supposed-to-be-friends were all doing as adults now. I left when I was 17 and now I was about to turn 25.

My thoughts were interrupted by the dorm P.A. system, "Mail call. Mail call. All inmates, listen up for your name. If it's called, come forward with your I.D."

Of course, I'm hoping I got mail just like everyone else in the dorm. My name gets called twice, so I pick up a letter from a Keith Edwards and an Ebony magazine with Vanessa Williams on the cover. As I walked back to my bunk, I heard someone say, "Can I read that Ebony when you done, home team?" I looked to my right to see who asked the question. It was Mater Head. I nodded my head and sat on my bunk to figure out who Keith Edwards was. I opened the letter and began to read it.

August 4, 1994
Yo wassup with you, Helimite. I know you probably thought
you wouldn't hear from me again. I been out five months
now. I didn't go back to Merritt Island, Florida. I'm in Ft.
Lauderdale working in a warehouse, operating a forklift.
My phone number is 954-725-6345. Call me when you can.
I'm ready to start the train. Stay up, man. Real recognize
real.
Hawk

All I could do was smile. Keith, a.k.a. Hawk was like a lieutenant
for me back at Polk C.I. He handled all the cocaine sales for me back then.
He really didn't have but two customers that bought it all every time. Two
Seminole Indians that lived in the dorm with him. It was very rare for a
recently released convict to sit down and write a letter and mail it off to the
chain gang, but Hawk was different. He was cut from a different cloth for
sure. How did he end up in Fort Lauderdale?

The night we connected at Polk C.I., I lived in C Dorm with him and
had never said a word to him because for one, I'm not friendly and two, he
was always with this skinny ass white kid who worked with the maintenance
crew at the prison. I was only 18 at the time and I had automatically assumed
they had some gay shit going on. Anyway, there was a loud discussion going
on between him and four other convicts about high school football, class 3A
and 4A. Hawk was boasting about the Merritt Island Mustangs. I was familiar with their program.

Once upon a time I lived on Merritt Island and ran track for the
Lewis Carrol Roadrunners. That year, the Mustangs went to the State Cham-
pionship. I can't recall if they won it all or not, but I do remember their star
running back's first name, Walt. I never knew his last name, but he lived on
the same street I lived on, School House Lane. I was in the third or fourth
grade back then and I used to run sprints and jog up and down School House
Lane to stay on point for the upcoming track meets. Walt would always
come outside to push me harder and encourage me.

I spoke up and said, "I remember them Merritt Island Mustangs with
Walt at running back."

Hawk looked at me and said, "I was the full back blocking for him."

By the size of Hawk's neck and shoulders, I believed him. His eyes
grew wide with excitement and his arms was up in the air. "How you know

about them Mustangs? I thought you was from Palm Beach County," he questioned.

"I used to live on Merritt Island on School House Lane, across the street from Ron and Robert Price."

Hawk became more interested in what I was saying as he scratched his head. "I stayed three houses down from the Price brothers. My mama has lived there twenty plus years."

I nodded my head up and down as he spoke. I ended up naming a few more people he knew, and now I was his homeboy from Merritt Island, even though I wasn't.

What I didn't know, at the time, was Hawk had a mule. That skinny white boy he was always around was going to the visitation park to visit some girl who would bring two ounces on Saturday and two on Sunday. That white boy would pack his ass and hand it all over to Hawk to control. Hawk would sell three and the other one he put in the atmosphere. Hawk used to point up to the clouds and say, "Helimite, look at them clouds up there. I think we need to get on they level." Then he would spark up a fat ass joint, right there on the spot.

Some known jackboys had caught wind that the skinny ass white boy was moving weed through the Visiting Park. So, me and my other home-boy Danky would wait outside the Visitation Park by the kitchen to escort the white guy back to his dorm. We would go to the bathroom area and act like we were washing our hands while he sat on the toilet and pushed them two ounces out, compressed and sealed with black tape. The package was the size of a dill pickle. He would wash it off with water and *Irish Spring* soap and hand it over to me. I would stash the packages that were received on Saturday and Sunday until Tuesday morning. That was the day officer Kool Moe "D" would work our dorm. I would slip him a 50-dollar bill then myself and Hawk would be clear to handle our business. We moved like that for almost four months.

One Monday morning, that skinny ass white boy was told he was being transferred to another prison. That was like a punch in the gut to Hawk. He couldn't hide the pain of losing a mule.

I looked over at him and said, "Hawk, don't worry bro. We will find a way to keep this train going."

It took a while, but I came across a C.O. who was interested in making some cash and the train was back on track.

CHAPTER 19

My days were long inside of this General Warehouse. Mr. Sneads moved around the warehouse constantly trying to watch my every move. There was a whole lot of stuff that carried some value to the inmate population, but they searched you coming in and out of this warehouse, which didn't matter to me because I wasn't interested in any of what the warehouse had in stock. I wasn't a thief. I was a hustler, and I wasn't about to lower my standards.

I still hadn't found a way to get myself removed from this job. As I sat there on a milk crate thinking, another semi-truck arrived and had to be unloaded. Once the driver backed all the way in and opened the doors, I saw that it was full of all kinds of supplies. I went and grabbed a dolly and waited for Mr. Sneads to give me direction on where he wanted the supplies placed. He came out of his office pulling his pants up and pulling down on his brown Department of Corrections baseball cap like he always did. He had an ink pen in his hand, ready to sign off on the truck driver's paperwork. I looked at the boxes I would be unloading and saw toilet paper, toothbrushes and toothpaste. Mr. Sneads advised me to put the toothbrushes and toothpaste on a shelf to my right and the toilet paper on a shelf to my left.

The voice in my head went to talking to me and I followed his lead and did as he told me to. I took the toothbrushes and toilet paper and put it on the shelf to my left and stacked all the toothpaste over to my right. By the time Mr. Sneads figured out I had stocked everything backwards, I was done and taking a water break. Mr. Sneads walked toward me, wiping the sweat from his forehead with a handkerchief.

"Inmate, Helimite," he yelled. "Why didn't you follow the simple direction I gave you with those stocking supplies?"

"I put everything away, sir, as nice and neat as a I could."

"Come with me," he instructed.

He took me to his office and wrote a C.C., a corrective consultation. It was pretty much like a warning on an official Department of Correction form saying I disobeyed a verbal order. He pushed the document towards me and told me to sign it.

I responded, "No sir. To sign that document would be me saying I'm in agreement with whatever you wrote."

He stood there fuming like he wanted to slap the shit outta my ass then stated, "What do you mean by 'with whatever I wrote'? Nobody's lying on you. Read it yourself before you sign it."

I shook my head from left to right and said, "Mr. Sneads, I'm not gonna read it because I can't read, sir. And I barely can write. I've been try-ing to get in the Education Department for a while now and the Classifica-tion Department keeps telling me I have too much time left on my sentence to go to school. They are holding the seats for inmates with ten years and under left on their sentence." The look on my face was of pure despair. I was trying my best to shed a tear.

Mr. Sneads looked at me, took his hat off and rubbed his skull and responded, "Young man, I'm gonna make a phone call to my friend, Mr. Ghostlon in Classification, and get you a seat in one of those classrooms. I wish you would have said something about this earlier. This explains why you stocked everything in the wrong locations."

He took the Corrective Consultation form and tore it into pieces and told me to go back to my assigned dorm for the rest of the day. "I can't use you in here if you can't read and write."

"Yes, sir. I understand."

He went back to his office and picked up his phone and I left and headed back to the dorm. I made it back a little after the 4 o'clock shift change. I went ahead and got in an early shower before the rest of the dorm arrived. I put on a pair of black and red Florida State shorts and a wife beater, a few swipes from my speed stick deodorant and some baby powder down the inside of my shirt. At that point I was so fresh and clean, for the penitentiary anyway.

I pulled my locker drawer open and pulled out the letter from Hawk. I read it again and decided to call him after the 5 p.m. count. It was extremely hot in this dorm. The baby powder I put on to stay cool and dry had already absorbed all the sweat it could, and I knew I would have to jump back into a cold shower before 10 p.m. to rinse off. I turned my radio on to the sounds of Craig Mack, *Brand New Flava in Ya Ear*. The beat was thumping in through my Pro 35 headphone set. It wasn't long before they announced count time, and two officers came through. To my surprise, count cleared in about 15 minutes.

I got up, put on my slides and went to the phone area. It was wide open. I picked up the receiver and looked at Hawk's letter again to make sure I dialed the right number. It rung twice and I could hear the Department of Corrections voice recording say, "You have a collect call from Helimite at Apalachee Correctional Institution. If you accept, push zero. To refuse, push 1."

As he pushed zero, I was connected and all I could hear was the Isley Brothers playing in the background. I spoke first, "Hawk, whassup home team?"

"My main man, Helimite. It's good to hear your voice."

"I can hear your voice better if you turn the Isley Brothers down."

He gave a short laugh and said, "Hold on."

The music faded and Hawk was back on the phone telling me about how life was so good for him as a free man in Broward County. He told me about his new girlfriend, Tasha from Jamaica, who was already pregnant and about his job as a forklift operator at Publix Warehouse.

I congratulated him on the baby that was on the way and the job. I tell him, "I'm just holding on by faith up here at A.C.I It's nothing like Polk C.I."

He said, "It's only one Polk C.I., Helimite. That spot and the breed of convicts that were there made that prison go! Anyway, my brother, when is your package permit month? I wanna show you some love."

All of a sudden, he started coughing out of control. "Hawk, you okay?"

"Yeah, Helimite, this weed down here so good I'm starting to believe they spraying this weed with something. It has me high for at least eight hours a day."

"Must be nice, Hawk. It's dry as a Sahara Desert here."

"It be that way sometimes, dude. It will get better later. Now tell me, what all you need on your package permit?"

"I need three v-neck shirts, a pair of winter pajamas, a pair of shoes, two sweatshirts. A blue one and a white one."

"What kind of shoes you want?"

"I don't care hawk. As long as it's a size 13."

"I gotcha, Helimite. Just keep your head up in there. I'll buy you all that stuff this Friday when I get paid. In the meantime, mail me your approved package permit slip ASAP."

"Okay, Hawk. I appreciate you reaching out to me, man."

"Helimite, real recognize real inside the joint and out."

I heard the volume go back up on the Isley Brothers at his crib. I laughed and said, "Hawk, you in love 'round there or what?"

He says, "Yeah! In love with this good sex. Tasha is from the animal planet, dog. Once we hit the bedroom, it's whatever!"

"Well, enjoy yourself, Hawk. You deserve it. All that time you did."

"I am. Call me, Helimite, once you receive your package."

"I will bro. Take care, Much love. Later." I hung up the phone and shook my head and laughed. Hawk said Tasha was from the animal planet. I never heard that one before. I gotta use that one. I sat down at one of the three all-wood card tables in the dorm. Half of the crowd is listening to the local news station on the T.V. screen. *What would I be doing right now if I was free?* That was the question the voice in my head had presented. Believe it or not, I didn't have a clue. I wasn't a teenager anymore. I was a grown ass man who had yet to develop or aggressively pursue a skill set. My homeboys Ant and Freddie Jay had graduated from that plumbing class and Rufus, last I heard, was taking an electrician class. I had more time than everybody else, so it wasn't meant to be right now due to them 55 years I was still at the front end of serving.

The noise from a stapler being used brought me back to reality. I turned my head to the left where the sound was coming from. Officer Tymes was at the bulletin board trying to staple all of the next day's callout sheets. Once he finally figured it out, I approached the board and looked for the job change sheet. I found it and all I could do was smile. It read, "Inmate Helimite FROM: General Warehouse TO: Education." Mr. Sneads had some major pull to get that done so quickly, just like that. I love it when a plan comes together. I guess I'll be getting my GED now.

I scanned over the rest of the callouts, and I was on there to see

Mental Health Department at 2 p.m. tomorrow. That put another smile on my face. I loved sittin' up in Dr. White's Office talking for hours, gazing into those beautiful eyes and watching her lick her lips so innocently but so seductive. I wondered if she knew that I was constantly lusting for her and masturbating with her in mind. I'm hard right now with the anticipation of my visit tomorrow.

75

CHAPTER 20

Third yard was always the yard the whole institution showed up for due to the sun going down. Today was no different. The weight cage was packed. Softball game was flooded with inmates and the basketball court was standing room only. It was, bring your best five to the court going to ten points by ones and three-pointers count as two. This would be my first time touching the court at A.C.I.

I walked up and shouted, "Who got next?"

Everybody looked at me like, ain't no way you gettin' on this court today. Way too many teams waiting.

"I got next!" I heard a familiar voice say. I see the midget Mater Head from Palm Beach emerge from the crowd.

"Let me get a run in, Mater Head."

He nodded his head up and down and said, "I gotcha."

I was standing courtside watching the game, sizing up all the different players for both teams. I could already see who the winner of the current game would be. The duo of Cartoon and Junkie Slim was way too much for the other team. Junkie Slim did a finger roll with his left hand that rolled off the rim, only to be caught by Cartoon and flushed back in with a two-hand dunk. They have way too much energy.

Cartoon never stopped talking shit. "This a blowout, y'all. 7-nothing is a blowout going to ten all across the world. Who got next?" He screamed. "Get a new five out here. We gonna run this court 'till they call the yard."

Mater Head walked out on the court, stretching.

Cartoon said, "Mater Head, how much Ben Gay you got on, man. Y'all don't smell that shit?"

Everybody had to laugh at that.

The court was a smooth concrete slab. The goals were at regulation height of ten feet. Most prisons, I had heard, were starting to raise their basketball rims to eleven and twelve feet to keep the high-flying ballers from tearing up the rims and backboards. This wasn't the case at Apalachee Correctional Institution.

Mater Head introduced me to the other three players on our team. Lee Lee from Palm Beach, Malik at 6'8 from Louisiana and Bump City from Miami. Mater Head and Lee Lee were the guards. I had the small forward spot, 6'8 at center, of course, and Bump City at the power forward position. The winner of the last game automatically had the ball first.

All the Super Two radios were tuned to the same radio station and the 69 Boys, *Tootsee Roll* was playing loud and clear, "...*cotton candy, sweet as gold, let me see you tootsee roll...*" And roll, they did at all four corners of that court. It be days like this I wish I could be back home playing ball with the cats I grew up with. Even though the atmosphere was laid back at the moment, this was still prison and was subject to change at any given time. The voice in my head screamed, *don't get caught up in the moment, Helimite, because you don't know these dudes.*

The game started with Junkie Slim shooting a three, which really wasn't a three but an alley-oop that Cartoon caught and dunked on Bump City. The crowd went into a frenzy with 'damns' and 'hell nawwws'.

Cartoon went back down court screaming, "He tall and that's all!"

I tell Malik, "If they get past Bump City, Malik. I need you to protect the rim."

He looked at me and said, "Yeah, I got him next time."

We came back down on offense and Mater Head and Lee Lee was passing the ball back and forth to each other. The next thing I know, Lee Lee is shooting a straight brick. Bump City grabs the rebound and puts it right back up off the backboard. We go back down court and fall into a 2-3 zone defense. These cats weren't shooting jumpers like that. They were trying to attack the rim and me and Bump City wasn't having it.

I fouled Cartoon every time he tried to slash through my side of the paint. "Ain't nothing over here, playa. You can shoot all the threes you want but this side of the paint is closed."

I was already dripping with sweat, and I was clearly out of basketball shape and was so glad to the see the basketball go out of bounds on a blocked shot by Bump City, so I could catch my breath. The other team wanted a fast-paced game. Normally, I would have been down for that but today, we need to turn this into a half-court game not a run and gun pace.

The score was six to four. Their lead. I can hear my baby Brandy singing about "...*she'll always be my best friend*," on the radio.

The ball is put back into play and one of the other dudes on Cartoon's team shoots a jump shot that misses terribly. Malik grabs the rebound and passes it to Bump City, who takes a few dribbles and passes it across the court to me. I catch and shoot a three-pointer. Count it! All net! The score is tied, 6-6 since a three-pointer only counts as two points. I can see all the outside dorm lights had just switched on, which meant only one thing. Security was about to close this rec yard for the day. In a pick-up game in prison, everybody knows whoever is leading when the P.A. system comes to life and says, "The yard is now closed. All inmates report to your assigned dorm for count," is declared the winner. So, it was important to not let these dudes get a last second shot off.

I screamed, "Time out," and huddled my team up. "They about to call yard, fellas."

Cartoon is screaming, "What y'all doing? Ain't no time outs in a pick-up game, especially if we have the ball."

Before any of us could respond, the P.A. System came to life. Game over. 6-6, tie. All I could say was *Thank You Lord* because I was tired.

======

The next morning, I woke up and my muscles were aching. I jumped in the shower to let the hot water work its magic. I got dressed for breakfast. The meal was creamed beef and potatoes, also known as "shit on a shank." How it acquired that name was before my time. The Chow Hall was packed. You had inmates jumping the wall to get back in line to eat twice. The wall was around four feet high, and these cats were clearing it no problem. I'll buy an extra tray before I jump the wall for another tray.

The white officer at the front of the line was being distracted on purpose by other inmates, claiming they didn't get no jelly on their trays, or a biscuit was missing. These boys knew how to work together when it came to that grocery.

I added salt and pepper to my food and started eating. Cartoon came and sat at my table and said, "Helimite, you got away yesterday. Make sure you show up last yard so we can run that back. It won't end in a tie today, playa."

I'm not ready for no rematch yet. I needed to do some jogging and some jumping jacks to get my wind back up. "Pass me that black pepper," I asked.

He handed it to me and said, "You need a job in a butcher shop, Helimite. All that choppin' you did last night. If we had a referee, you would have fouled out first quarter."

I laughed at that and responded, "If we had a fifth of liquor, we both would be dead drunk right now."

"That's a lie, Helimite. I don't drink or smoke."

"Well, what you do, Cartoon?"

"I recruit. Organize. Strategize. Get money."

"Well, do what you do, I can't help or hurt you."

"Helimite, you never know. Stay open-minded to networking with me and stop using my age for not wanting to. I can learn from you, and you can learn from me."

This 17-year-old kid was well before his time with his intellect and people skills. I picked up my tray and said, "Let's see what time reveals in this spot, Cartoon. I'll be here for a minute." I gave him a fist bump and we walked back to the dorm.

I brushed and flossed my teeth and got dressed for my first day of school at A.C.I. The 8 a.m. shift came in and fifteen minutes later the intercom system announced, "Work call. Work call. All inmates report to your morning job assignments."

I took my eye drop bottle and squeezed out two drops cologne. It was a must that I didn't smell like everyone else. That was one of the first steps of separation in a world where everybody wore blue uniforms with a white stripe going down the leg.

CHAPTER 21

It had been three weeks since I spoke to Hawk. I sent my approved package permit to him as he requested and I was curious to see what kind of shoes he would buy, since I left that totally up to him. It was no longer sunny days in A.C.I. It was mostly overcast a lot, between 50 to 60 degrees, and winter was right around the corner. You could actually see the season change up here in Sneads, Florida. The leaves falling, the trees going naked, but the smell from the chicken farm would not be denied. It was a constant.

I was making my way to the Law Library to check out what new law had passed and if any applied to my situation, when the P.A. system announced, "Attention on the compound. The following named inmates, report to the Property Room." A list of about 15 inmates were called and my name was included. I changed my route to head to the Property Room. When I arrived, there were six people already in line. I leaned back against the iron railing leading up to the property window and thought about Dr. White's fine ass. I know she looked forward to our sessions as much as I did, but she would never admit it. Her body language said it all and as R. Kelly once sang, "...*her body's calling*..." Dr. White's bangin' body was always calling for Helimite's attention. I was at the point now where I really was ready to ask her to let me get my freak on. My mind was already drifting on how I would suck on her breasts.

The sound of other inmates approaching the line brought me back to

80

reality. As I turned to see how the line was progressing, I now only had two people ahead of me. Picking up package permits was always like Christmas in here. I watched as one inmate walked by me with a hand full of new clothing items sent from home. Dude had a *kool-aid* smile on his face that only love from home could establish.

When I finally made it to the window, I handed the female property sergeant my I.D. card. She moved a few boxes around and found one with my name and prison number on it. She placed it on a table and used a box cutter to cut it open. I looked around the inside of the property room and there were packages everywhere, barely enough room for her to walk around in. She took out three v-neck tshirts from my box and said, "Whatever they sprayed these shirts with smells awesome."

I nodded my head up and down and said, "I have no idea, sarge. I'll ask when I call home."

She removed some pajamas, a pair of apple green canvas Converse tennis shoes and two sweatshirts. She put on gloves and searched every item then handed them to me. The shirts smelled like *Obsession* cologne. I wasn't for sure though. Hawk knew I played basketball so I really didn't know why he would send a pair of apple green, no ankle support canvas Converse All-Stars. I should have told him Nikes. I guess he sent what he could afford, so I need to be grateful for the love he showed, and tell the voice in my head to shut up.

I walked down the main walkway of the compound headed back to the dorm to secure my property in my locker, and then I'd circle back to the Law Library as originally planned. I could sit in the Law Library for hours at a time reading all the different cases around the world where justice wasn't being served. It appeared to be an agenda, more than anything, to lock up as many people as they could, especially people of color, to create jobs and other opportunities to profit from our incarceration.

Me, on the other hand, was guilty as charged in my situation. But the amount of time – 55 years – was and still is an illegal sentence that I needed to fight to the end. I'm not spending 55 years in here when I'm not required to. I missed my mama and sisters so much. There's way too much going on out there in free society for me not to be around to support them and have their back. Lord, I need you to make a way. The stress was building. I would love to smoke me a joint right now but that looked like and felt like mission impossible way up here at A.C.I.

I entered the front office of the schoolhouse and I must say it felt good. All the school staff was warm and bubbly. I noticed they didn't even keep an officer assigned to the school. You would think that with all the female staff working here, it would be mandatory to have a male officer present. I guessed that since the security building was right across the sidewalk from the Education Department, the staff felt that they were secure.

I walked in with a smile on my face and all the staff there were polite and cheerful. If it wasn't for the beige and brown paint on the walls reminding me that this was the Department of Corrections, this place would easily pass as an education building in free society.

I was greeted with, "Good morning. How can I assist you?" A young, brown skin secretary asked. She didn't look like she was old enough to buy beer, let alone work inside of a prison.

"Yes. My name is Helimite. I was on the job change sheet yesterday."

She reached for some paperwork and checked my name off a list. She walked from behind her desk and asked me to follow her. As we walked, she asked, "What is the last grade you completed?"

I thought back for a minute and finally responded, "The 10th grade."

She opened the door to a classroom where there were about twelve other students. She invited me to have a seat. I sat down at a desk toward the front of the classroom. She handed a thin folder with my name on it to an older white female teacher, who stood up from behind her desk with a pair of blue jeans on that clung to every curve her body possessed. She introduced herself as Mrs. Whitmore and explained that everyone in the class will be taking a T.A.B.E. The Test of Adult Basic Education was administered to see who was ready to be placed in a pre-GED classroom and who would need more time schooling before they could be placed in pre-GED.

Mrs. Whitmore passed out the test booklets to everyone present, along with a number two pencil. She explained that every section was timed. "Do the best you can for now and don't worry about stuff you don't know. Don't raise your hand once the testing starts because I'm not allowed to help you with any of the questions or math problems. If anyone needs to use the restroom or take a smoke break, you have fifteen minutes to take care of all of that right now."

With that being said, the whole classroom stood up and walked toward the front door, into a courtyard with a few picnic tables and benches. A bunch of inmates and staff were scattered all over the courtyard, so this had to be the designated break time for the entire Education Department.

Many inmates were smoking cigars and cigarettes while others stood around telling lies about the lifestyle they left in society. There was a small group of inmates surrounding a picnic table. As I approached them, I could hear the bang of hands-on-wood keeping rhythm while two young boys rapped about the finer things in life. They had a nice flow going and the crowd that surrounded them were bobbing to the beat. A bell rang and everything came to a stop, and everyone went back to the classrooms where they came from.

I never had an issue with going to school while in society. I went to Lincoln Elementary, John F. Kennedy Junior High School, and then on to North Shore High School. I stayed suspended, often for fighting. But when I wasn't on suspension, I thrived in the classroom. Reading and comprehension was always a strong area for me. History class was always one-sided on who discovered or invented something. I mean, everyone has a brain, but the way history is being taught to my generation, it only glorified one race of people.

I made my way back to my seat in the classroom and sat down. I couldn't help but reminisce about them good ole days. Adidas and Fila warm-up suits. Run DMC playing on just about every car stereo. Gangster rap was non-existent back then. I was brought back to the present at the sound of the teacher's voice explaining how much time we had on this portion of the T.A.B.E. test. As she dropped the test booklet on my desk and walked past me, I couldn't resist the opportunity to look back at all that thickness in those jeans. The teacher, suddenly, turned around to look behind her and pretty much saw the whole class lusting at the curves and shape of her body.

Her face was flushed as she took one hand and ran it through her hair. "I need you guys to focus on this test and not on me. I'm flattered but not to the extent that I would ever date someone who didn't have an education. Getting your GED will help you in every aspect of your life once you're free again." She looked around the classroom slowly, I guess, to make sure her message was received loud and clear. She looked at one inmate in a far corner and said, "Put that thing away. If I see it out again, I will have you removed from this class and placed in administrative confinement."

I was sitting at my desk trying to figure out if I really just heard the teacher ask an inmate to put his dick up. Any other prison, he would be in a world of trouble. Officers would be coming from every direction to hog tie his ass up. I guess this teacher really wanted to see this dude get his GED.

CHAPTER 22

The three hours of T.A.B.E. testing was finally over, and I must admit, I didn't know or didn't remember any of that stuff on the test. I hadn't been in school since 1987. I guessed at a lot of the questions and problems presented on the test. I took a deep breath, sighed with relief to get out of the classroom and headed to my mental health call out with Dr. Linda White.

When I entered the Mental Health Building, the first thing I noticed was that there was no officer present to greet me or pat search me. A secretary asked me who I was and who I was there to see. She picked up a phone and dialed Dr. White's number and said, "Dr. White, your patient Helimite has arrived."

I was sitting in the lobby saying to myself, *patient? She called me a patient?* The voice in my head said that *these people think you're crazy for real.*

Over half of the prison population is, or is pretending to be crazy to get that *Thorazine* prescribed to them to stay high, all natural day, while serving time. This secretary doesn't know you or your mental state of mind. What she does know is that your ass is not here for choir practice or church *so get out your feelings, Helimite, and keep playing the game. You say you're a boss player, right? Well, play on player.* I'm nodding my head slowly in agreement with the voice in my head. I normally tell it to shut up but today it was reciting truth and knowledge on my brain.

The phone ringing in the lobby broke the silence. The secretary answered then raised her head and said, "Dr. White is ready for you now."

I stood up, gave myself a look over and walked down the hall toward Dr. White's office. No escort today. Something must have happened at a neighboring prison, or the officers must have had a mandatory training today. I've been incarcerated long enough to know how security moves and operates. For security to be absent here and in the Education Department was out of the ordinary. I arrived at Dr. White's office and knocked softly on her door. I heard music playing faintly in the background. It sounded like Chaka Khan, *What Cha' Gonna Do for Me.*

Dr. White opened the door and stepped to the side for me to pass. "Good afternoon, Dr. White," I announced, to break the silence.

"What's so good about it, inmate Helimite? Oh, I forgot, it's Convict Helimite."

"Whatever you're comfortable with, Dr. White."

She had the afro picked out to perfection with a black and red floral print dress that hugged and clung to her body just right. As she moved to take a seat behind her desk her backside moved up and down with ease, no restriction at all. The voice in my head screamed, *Helimite, this chick don't have no panties on.* The fabric of this dress was not see-through but was made of lightweight material, for sure.

"Helimite!"

I refocused my attention at hearing my name.

Dr. White continued, "What's so good about this afternoon?"

"Well, the sun is shining, Dr. White. I have my health and strength still available to me, so I'm grateful for that part. But in other areas, I must admit it is a struggle and a process I am so unfamiliar with."

She leaned forward with her hands clasped together on her desk and asked me to speak freely. My legs were shaking from side to side, more out of habit than nervousness. I cleared my throat and said, "I've been hearing voices a lot lately, Dr. White."

She reached for a pen and yellow tablet and said, "When did you first start hearing voices, Helimite?"

"I really can't recall the actual day it started but it's starting to overwhelm me, at times."

"What are the voices saying to you, Helimite?"

I shrugged my shoulders, still shaking my left leg from side to side and said, "It depends on what's going on at the moment."

She wrote something on her yellow tablet then shifted in her seat like she was getting more comfortable to take in a long story. "When was the last time this voice spoke to you?"

I paused for a moment, inhaled and exhaled, and looked directly at her. "About ten minutes ago, Dr. White."

"And what did it say to you?"

I held eye contact with her and said, "The voice said that you probably don't have any panties on and that your pussy is probably shaved clean and that you have no stretch marks anywhere around them hips, ass, and thighs."

She held eye contact the whole time. She bit down on her bottom lip, slightly, and wrote something down again on her yellow tablet and asked, "Is that it, Helimite?"

"No, it isn't. The voice said that you not being fucked right at home, and you need someone who's really going to appreciate that pussy and cater to it like it's a warm bowl of peach cobbler, fresh out the oven."

The room was so quiet. I could hear her breathing quicken. She took her right hand and placed it on the side of her face and looked at me. "Helimite, do you ever talk back to or respond to this voice?"

"Yes. Sometimes I tell it to shut up or I might say, 'you dead ass right,' and let the voice continue its opinion."

She nodded her head up and down and said, "I see," and writes on the yellow tablet again. She gently scratched her head like she was in deep thought. "I'm going to tell you what I think, Helimite. I believe you have TWYD, which is spreading kinda fast all over the U.S. right now."

"TWYD?" I repeat. "What, actually, is it, Dr. White, and is it curable?"

"In some cases, yes, and some cases, no. It depends on how deeply it's rooted." She scooted her chair back from her desk and walked to the front of her desk and stood directly in front of me. She pulled out a small white beeper looking device with a black button in the middle and asked, "Do you know what this device is, Helimite?"

I shook my head from left to right, my left eyebrow raised, and said, "I've never seen one before."

She raised it higher and said, "This device has been issued to all the employees in the Florida Department of Corrections. It's a panic button or emergency response device. If I were to press this button, at least 20 officers would be in my office in a matter of minutes. This device means that there is no need to station any officer in this building anymore, or any other building where female staff are assigned. I don't want to have to use this device on you, Helimite, but I will. I don't believe for one minute that you're hearing voices. But I do believe you have made your first and last attempt to try and play on my intelligence."

I interrupted her, "You just stated that I have TWYD."

"Oh, you absolutely have TWYD, Helimite, which stands for Thinking With Your Dick! Now, don't interrupt me again."

The voice in my head screamed, *your freaky ass going to jail/ confinement, Helimite.* I ignored the voice and listened to Dr. White speak. "If you refuse to follow any of my next instructions that I'm about to give you, I promise you, I'm pressing the panic button."

CHAPTER 23

"Do you understand, Helimite?"

"Yes, ma'am!" I quickly responded.

"Good. Now, let's continue."

She took a step towards me and adjusted my legs to stand between them. She placed her hands on the arms of my chair and as she leaned over my left shoulder, she whispered in my ear, "So, you like to play, Helimite? Let's play then."

I was nervous for real. I didn't know what to expect. My heart was beating so hard and fast. There's no way she couldn't hear it nearly exploding out of my chest. I felt the tip of her nose touch my neck. She inhaled my cologne like she was snorting a line of cocaine then she exhaled slowly with the softest moan I've ever heard. Everything in me wanted to throw her ass across that desk and stick this dick in her but I remembered that emergency device and had to sit my ass still. She stood back up and took a few steps back. She commanded me very matter-of-factly not to move or say one word.

"Just watch me," she said in a low whisper.

She unbuttoned her dress, one button at a time. Her eyes locked in on mine.

"Now that we know you're not hearing voices, let me add some visuals to those thoughts in your head."

As her dress fell to the floor and my eyes left hers to take in the sight of her body, I quickly realized every thought I had about her body was on point and she wore no panties. Her cocoa butter brown skin looked soft. Breast, supple. Stomach, flat. Thighs, thick. Ass so fat I could see it from the front and not a stretch mark in sight.

She stepped out of her dress. Heels still on. She slowly, seductively walked toward her desk. She gently sat on the edge of it. "Helimite, position your chair so you are sitting directly in front of me."

I did exactly as she requested and at this point, for the first time in my life, all the blood in my body rushed from my dick to my tongue. My mouth watered at the sight before me. *Stay focused, Helimite*, the voice in my head screamed. *Play it cool.*

She placed her left leg on the right arm of my chair and leaned back her right hand. "Follow my hand," she whispered. Her left hand caressed her breast and slowly slid down her stomach to her pussy. I thought to myself, *I know she's not about to make me watch her play with herself.* She massaged her clit and slid her middle finger inside her crevice. I could hear the squish. She was already wet. When she pulled her finger out, I could see her moistness glistening on it. She placed that finger in her mouth and moaned as she slowly pulled it out.

"Mmmm," she moaned. "Taste me," she said as she motioned for me to get closer to her.

Y'all know I'm not into eating pussy like that but I absolutely had no choice. She gave the order. She was in control right now. I licked, I sucked, and kissed on her clit like my life depended on it.

Dr. White reached out and grabbed the back of my head and moved and grinded closer to my face. She moaned, "That's it. Right there. I like that."

After at least ten minutes of me tongue lashing her, I stood up to see my erection trying to burst through my prison blues uniform. I quickly undid my buttons and freed my hardness and drove it right into her warm and wet love tunnel. I braced both my hands on her desk and kept a steady and strong drive in and out of her body. She wrapped her arms around my neck and told me to stop but I knew she had to mean, "Don't stop," because of how tight she had both arms wrapped around me. I kept on stroking, and she repeated twice more for me to stop, but I knew she didn't mean because of the way she was holding on to me. So, I pushed deeper inside of her. I was enjoying the pleasures of her body when a faucet of warm water splattered up against my stomach running down my body to the floor. I stared at Dr. White in disbelief, and she returned my stare.

She stated matter-of-factly, "I told you to stop."

I moved away from her to gather myself. I used my boxer shorts like a towel and dried myself off. She moved back behind her desk and wiped herself off as well. She dressed herself and straightened her hair out. I moved the chair I was sitting in back to where it originally was and sat down and glared at Dr. White and I shrugged my shoulders, hands raised like, 'what the fuck.'

"What? I told you to stop," Dr. White scolded. "So, don't look at me like that. As a matter of fact, you're dismissed for today, Helimite. I may or may not be here next week. If I am, I will put you on the call-out."

I stood up and grabbed the doorknob to leave her office with no other words. I'm hot as fish grease walking back to the dorm where I would most definitely be one of the first people in the shower. I had heard and read in porn magazines before about her kind and type but never imagined a Black girl to be into all that. I was mad because I didn't bust a nut, and I was mad because she felt the need to piss all over me. A golden shower is what they called it in those porn magazine sex stories, I used to read.

I entered the dorm and headed to my bunk. I opened my locker, pulled out a honeybun and spread peanut butter on top of it and bit into it. I pressed the on button to my Super 2 Radio hoping some music would clear my head some. An old school jam by Rick James was on and he sang about *"...a very freaky girl. The kind you don't take home to mother..."*

CHAPTER 24

8 p.m. count had just cleared and one of my favorite shows, Moesha, was on T.V. I was late getting to the TV Room so there was absolutely nowhere for me to sit down. Both phones were wide open so I figured I might as well use that time to give Hawk a call and thank him for sending me that package permit.

The last thing Hawk said in his letter was, "Real recognize real, Helimite. I gotcha." You meet and come in contact with so many different walks of life in here. Trying to figure out who is real and who is pretending can be challenging. But once again, real will always reveal itself in movement and in pressure situations. Money doesn't make you real – it's just paper that affords you to buy things you need and want. Real comes from within your DNA.

Hawk helped me make thousands of dollars back at Polk Correctional Institution and at the same time blessed himself with a good stash of cash for his release date. Back then, the Department of Corrections was only giving you $200 dollars and a bus ticket to re-enter society, which was basically, nothing.

I picked up the phone and dialed Hawk's number. He answered on the third ring. "You have a collect call from Helimite at Apalachee Correctional Institution. To accept, dial one…" Hawk pushed one and the first thing I heard was slow music, again. This time it was Johnny Gill's, *There You Go.*

"How you doin', Hawk?"

"All is well, bro. Life is good for me on this side of the fence. I have no complaints."

"All you play is slow music around there, Hawk?"

He immediately started laughing and said, "Hell naw, Helimite. I been bumpin' Too Short and Tupac all day, but I have to switch it up once night falls, bro."

"I feel ya, Hawk. I'm just messin' with you. I was calling to thank you for the package permit you sent. I received it two days ago. You had the Property Room sarge in love with that cologne you sprayed on them v-neck t-shirts. What was the name of that cologne?"

Hawk answered, "That was Cool Water. It still be turnin' heads. My girl loves it."

"Cool Water? I never heard of that one before."

His response was a stream of heavy coughing.

"Hawk, you alright? You sick or something?" I asked.

"I'm good. Just blowing these good trees they have on these Fort Lauderdale streets."

"Must be nice," I commented.

Hawk quickly responded, "What you mean, 'must be nice,' Helimite? I know you doing your one-two-step by now."

"It's not that type of party up here in hillbilly land, Hawk. I told you last time we talked." The constant smell of the chicken farm across the road made sure you never forgot that you're in hillbilly land.

Hawk asked, "Helimite. Listen. Do you remember Bloodhound and K-Mite from Miami?"

I answered, "Yes. They were at Polk C.I. with us back in '89. They used to get that fire ass weed. The bags used to have a stamp on them. 'Judah,' with a lion head or bags with 'Door Bell' stamped on them."

"Yeah, that's right! Now, do you remember the route they used to get it in?"

At that moment a light switch came on in my head. I responded, "Hell yeah, I remember."

"Okay then, call me tomorrow and lace me up on what you think." Hawk suggested.

A wide grin expanded across my face. "Alright, bro. I'll do that. Have a good night. Later."

I placed the phone down and walked back to my bunk. I opened the locker and just stared at the apple green converse tennis shoes. I removed them from out of my locker, climbed in my bed with them and placed them under my covers. I sat back for a minute and thought back to how Blood-hound and K-Mite used to have brand new shoes taken to a shoe shop in Miami and have them broke down and rebuilt with all kinds of drugs, professionally hid on the inside of the shoe. I don't ever remember them using a pair of canvas converse tennis shoes, though.

They used the suede buck boots with the dice on the side. The boot heels were stuffed and resewn together. They would bring the shoes to my barbershop on the south end at Polk C.I. to bust the shoe down. A pair of Converses was never in that bust-down lineup.

I wanted to wait till lights out at 10 p.m. to see what was up but I was way too excited and curious at the same time. I ran my hand inside of the right shoes and of course felt nothing unusual. I dug into the outside of the insole and pulled really hard. I heard whatever glue that was used to seal it breaking free. The whole insole released. I turned it over to examine it and to my surprise, on everything I love, it was a long Hershey bar looking block, compressed and seated inside where the rubber padding would normally be, from the front of the shoe to the back. They left enough rubber on the outside of the insole to be able to glue everything back in. This shoe was done so professional I almost couldn't believe it. Except, here was this shoe.

I opened my locker and pulled out a cigar box I kept miscellaneous stuff in. Nail clipper, ink pens, postage stamps, paper clips, etc. I dumped all the items out and into my locker and then proceeded to pull the package free from the insole. It had aluminum foil around it and clear wrap sealing it on the outside.

I broke into the package with my fingernails and could immediately smell the aroma of that good Broward County weed that Hawk had been talking about and, coughing to, for weeks now. I dumped it into the cigar box and closed the lid. The weed looked just like parsley. It had been put in a blender or something. None of it was budded up. I'm pretty sure I had at least two ounces in this one size 13 shoe. My heart raced and my brain ran numbers on the money I was about to make.

I picked up my headphones and turned my radio on. The rap song by Luniz was playing, *"I got five on it… messing with that indo weed."* I laughed to myself and said, *these people at the radio station here gotta be watching me and making a soundtrack to my life movement at the same time.*

All I could think about now was Dr. White. Her fine ass would be in a world of trouble the next time I saw her. She had never interviewed or counseled with a high Helimite before. I planned on smoking a fat one and then adding *Visine* to my eyes to keep the red out. I'm normally Mack-a-roni when we conversate, but on some good weed, I am the mack and the roni and some cheese!

CHAPTER 25

The TABE test results were in. Test of Adult Basic Education. I had scored high enough on it to be placed in the pre-GED classroom. I walked into my classroom and met my new teacher, Mrs. Bryant. She was a brunette in her late 30's. She had a nice personality and was easy to talk to. She kept a coffee pot in her classroom and every time she fixed a cup she would say, "I like my men just like my coffee. Black and strong!" It surprised me how blunt and straight forward she was, especially pertaining to her preference in the men she dated.

The red brick classroom was cold and stuffy. This prison was so old I wondered if the heat even worked. I continued to look the classroom over while I waited for my turn to be briefed by Ms. Bryant. After ten minutes of watching all these different characters, who were clearly my classmates now, I heard my name called.

"Inmate Helimite."

"Yes ma'am. Right here."

"Can you come to my desk, please?"

I rose from my seat and walked to the front of the classroom to Ms. Bryant's desk. She looked me over, grinned and said, "Relax. You're not in any trouble, Helimite. This is a safe zone for growing and learning. Your education will open many doors and opportunities in the future for you if you choose to lock in and focus."

She explained to me that my math scores needed to increase in order to obtain my GED. "I'll be assigning one of my aides to assist you with this to get you up to par."

She leaned over and pulled one of her desk drawers open and removed a thick ass GED book that had to be bullet proof. It was so thick! She handed it to me and said, "Carlton will be your assigned aide. He will be here shortly. I have him picking up copies from the front office right now." Our pre-GED classroom supposedly had four inmate teacher's aides, who had already passed the GED test with outstanding test scores.

So, I walked back to my desk and sat down. *Carlton?* I say to myself. All I can think about is the nerdy character, Carlton, from the sitcom The Fresh Prince of Bel-Air. I sat there for a few minutes reading and flipping through the pages in the GED book while I waited for square-ass Carlton to show up. I heard the classroom door open but never looked up to see who entered. I was too stuck on an algebra problem.

I always *hated* algebra but *respectfully* knew I had to learn it to pass it and move forward. I doubted that I'd ever use algebra in a real-life situation. Reading and comprehension was my strong point. I really didn't like math but being a hustler, it was a must that I know how to add, subtract and multiply. I took in the lion's share on any product I hustled so I never had to divide nothing! And I never ever rounded off to the nearest hundred. Whoever thought of that had to be high. 96 dollars is 96 dollars. I can't round up to a hundred when I go to buy any product but then again, what did I know? I was a young man in his early 20's, deep off in the Florida Department of Corrections.

I'm going over past events in my life that eventually led me to this place and moment in time when I heard my name called again by my Ms. Bryant. "Helimite!"

"Yes, ma'am."

"Can you raise your hand so Carlton can see where your desk is?"

I raised my hand. To my surprise, Carlton is a.k.a. Cartoon. He looked at me with this smirk on his face, laughed, and said, "Well, well, well, Helimite. Look how the tables have turned."

I'm at a loss for words for a few seconds and finally said, "Good morning, Carlton."

That took the smile off his face as he responded, "Cartoon to you, if you want the blueprint to passing the GED test."

I looked at this 17-year-old kid and youth offender who already had his GED and nodded my head, yes.

"Step into my office, Helimite," he said as he moved to the back of the classroom to a long table in the back corner. We sat down and he said, "It's crazy how we just had a conversation at breakfast the other day. How you felt someone younger than you couldn't teach you anything. Now my question to you is, are you gonna be open-minded to receiving the information and knowledge I have for you to pass this test?"

I stared at him for a moment and took a deep breath and responded, "Hell yeah. But don't expect me not to dunk on your young ass or give you one of them good hard fouls when you try to come to the hoop for a layup."

He laughed and said, "Vice versa, Helimite."

It's my turn to laugh now and I said, "Let's get it, bro."

For the next two hours, Carlton simplified everything that I had recently thought was difficult in the GED book. I was headed in the right direction with my education. It would only be a matter of time now. I had three months to get ready for this exam.

=====

The weather was really taking a turn here in Sneads, Florida. It was getting extremely cold, and Thanksgiving and Christmas was right around the corner. I had been already campaigning to my mama to stop by and see me on her way to visit Grandma in Shellman, Georgia.

Me and Cartoon was still working in the classroom together. I had another month left before I could actually take the test. Outside of the classroom, we worked out together religiously inside the weight cage. Our favorite saying was, *ONLY THE STRONG GOES HOME* because the weak get raped, robbed, and end up in a body bag.

I wasn't playing too much ball because of the cold weather. I'm from south Florida where it never gets cold. The wind stayed whistling through the prison compound, carrying the stink of the chicken farm with it. I'm a long way from Palm Beach County and can't see what positive avenues I can take to get to a prison closer to home.

There were a lot of inmates here from up north who felt right at home, and they clearly outnumbered the south Florida population. They knew it and flexed it from time to time. Numbers don't lie or hide inside a prison, yet numbers don't decide or justify if one survived to see another day in here. Either you stay in your lane, know what you know, and do what you do. The Bible says be careful for nothing and that spoke volumes to me.

I'm hoping things can continue to remain peaceful here. I have a lot going on in my favor that I don't want to end anytime soon, but you just never know when the volcano will erupt. It's crazy but it's the reality of prison. I just pray it doesn't come to that at A.C.I. because Dorothy Mae Jones' son has a date with society one day that I intend to make by any means necessary. With that thought in mind, I need me another pipe just in case I needed to beat some sense into one of these damn fools around here.

CHAPTER 26

Time stands still for no one, and the days and weeks seemed to be flying by. I was making money with the help of Hawk. I was buying and using all the package permits of inmates who had no family to send them shoes, pajamas, sweatshirts, etc. There were so many pairs of Converse All Stars being worn at the prison. Now, I never told anyone the drugs were coming into the prison inside them shoes. That was my best kept secret. I would get the shoes, take the package out, stuff toilet paper where the package used to be carved in the shoe, super glue the sole back in and then sell or give the shoes away.

The Converse tennis shoes was being worn everywhere now, to the point that the staff was starting to believe everyone who had a pair was part of a gang. In a way, they were partly right. Most of the shoes were being sold or given to cats from down south, but I wasn't in no gang. I was part of a one-man gang. Nothing more. Nothing less. I sat back and watched the movement in the dorm every night, high as a kite, listening to the quiet storm hoping they would play some Anita Baker or Stephanie Mills. I could really zone out and push my pen to paper with the right music playing.

I'll never forget the night I went to the bathroom to smoke a joint. I was sitting on the toilet like I was taking a dump, and this dark-skinned brother came and sat on the toilet, literally right next to me. So, I tell him,

"Dude, why you passed all them toilets to sit next to me?"

He said, "I need to talk to you, and I don't need anybody in my business."

I tell him to move over to the next toilet – to put more separation between us. "Speak your mind."

He said, "My name is Dance-All-Night. I'm from Polk County. I wanna buy a 20-cent piece of weed."

"Do you have 20-dollar cash or canteen?"

"Canteen."

I tell him, "When I get done in here, I'll point you in the right direction."

He agreed and left the bathroom.

I shook my head and mumbled, *Dance-All-Night? Out of all the nicknames I've heard, this took the cake.*

I smoked the rest of my joint and flushed the roach. I spotted Dance-All-Night sitting on his bunk with what appeared to be 20 dollars' worth of cigarettes, which was like cash money, to an extent. I told my homeboy Mater Head to fix me two dime bags. My scary ass never kept or held anything on me. Once he finished, I pointed out Dance-All-Night and I climbed back in bed to listen to my music and write letters.

I wrote my mama to campaign for a Christmas visit again and I finally got around to writing Tasha, Hazellee, Octavia and Kooley C back. It had to be at least 3 a.m. when I got up to go take a piss. Out of the corner of my eye, I saw some movement that startled me. To my surprise, it was Dance-All-Night drenched in sweat, dancing his ass off at three in the morning all by himself. I laughed to myself and kept moving toward the bathroom. I had drunk way too much Tang earlier in the day and felt like I was going to bust.

I used the bathroom, climbed back up to my top bunk and lay there deep in thought. My body was tired from my daily workouts with Cartoon, but my mind never got any rest. I was always moving, planning, and scheming on how to make my situation better, inside and out. I was making a lot of money so I had to save as much as I could to be able to help myself and the people I loved outside the fence.

My bunk partner below me, who I knew from South Florida Reception Center was named Beach Boy. He was **Quiet As Kept** doing a life sentence. I never asked him what he did to get a life sentence because it wasn't my business. He was g-code on how he did his time, so I trusted him to handle certain stuff for me – like paying for and making sure I received the pipe I ordered from them white boys in the maintenance shop. I had seen and bought a few knives already but had to have my pipe as my main weapon. That pipe gets and keeps separation once it becomes visible.

Beach Boy was like my head of security. He kept one of the sharpest ice picks I have ever seen. I had heard through the grapevine a bunch of fiberglass knives would be available soon. With the fiberglass knives, you could walk through any metal detector all day strapped and not get detected.

The gang activity was pushing itself to the forefront of things. The gang called Folk Nation had killed, I repeat, killed another gang member from the Aryan Nation. This was so crazy to me. To an extent, you would think you were safe from those kinds of violent acts in prison, but truth be told, on any given day, you could get caught up and your life could be hanging in the balance. The officers here were afraid of the inmates. We greatly outnumbered them, and they were exposed and reachable to be touched all the time with the way these old ass dorms were built.

The ceiling fan above was squeaking and struggling like hell to spin around and around, adding no relief at all from the stale cigarette-smelling dorm. My eyes were getting heavier by the minute. Sleep would have me in a choke hold soon.

Now as I lay down to sleep.
I pray to the Lord my soul to keep.
If I should die before I wake,
I pray to the Lord, my soul to take.
In Jesus name. Amen.

CHAPTER 27

I woke up the next morning to the sound of a bunk bed being moved across the concrete floor. It was a loud screeching sound due to steel sliding over concrete. It was way too early in the morning for all this movement. Somebody needed their ass cussed out, but as I paid more attention to what the inmates were doing I had to **respect** it. They were putting tape over and across all the broken windows in the dorm to try and keep all that 30-degree weather from blowing inside, and they had to move the bunkbeds in order to get to the windows. I, personally, *hated* feeling these cold drafts blowing through all day long.

There was no way I could go back to sleep, so I rose up and let my feet hit the floor. I opened my locker and grabbed my toothbrush and toothpaste along with my washcloth and walked to the bathroom to kill that morning dragon that was on my tongue. As I brushed my teeth, I looked over the dorm and to my left, I saw dudes in between two bunks, getting tattoos done and to my right, a guy sitting on a five-gallon bucket was getting his hair cut with a comb and a razor. The hustle never stopped in the prison system. I washed my face and went back to my locker to put my hygiene items away. I pulled out two packs of apple-cinnamon oatmeal along with a bowl and spoon and walked over toward the hot water device. I added hot water to my oatmeal and stirred it up and attached the lid to the bowl to keep the heat in so the oatmeal could thicken up.

I saw a few guys shooting dice up against the wall next to the mop closet. I see Cartoon approaching the dice game with ten packs of tobacco in his hands. He hands the ten packs to the guy that's shooting the dice, and says, "I need 15 packs back on Wednesday."

The guy shooting dice said, "Like clockwork, Cartoon. I'll have the 15 packs to you on Wednesday."

Cartoon then looked over at me and said, "What you need, po' ass nigga?"

I looked back at him and said, "Some freedom. I'm tired of waking up and looking at all you ugly ass, hard-headed mutha fuckas every day."

"I can't help you with that, Helimite, but just know rain, snow, or shine, I'm always on my grind."

"I hear you Cartoon. Just be ready to grind inside that weight cage in 30 minutes."

"You asking me or telling me, Helimite?" Cartoon responded with a look on his face like he knew something I didn't. "Only the strong make it home, so don't meet me there. Beat me there."

I laughed and said, "You rhyming good this morning, Cartoon. You should have been a rapper instead of a thug running around the Ivey Lane projects."

He looked over his shoulder at me and said, "Birds of a feather 'rock' together. That's one thing I know. Hustlers hang with hustlers. Killers hang with killers."

"Yes, sir, Cartoon," I said while removing the lid off my bowl of oatmeal.

I refused to get up at 5:30 in the morning to go eat breakfast in 30-degree weather. But working out and training in that type of cold weather made me feel solid to the core. It really gets the blood flowing and you can't break a sweat in it because it was too cold. Cartoon never missed an opportunity to work out. All he wanted to do was train to get bigger and stronger, to eventually beat up all the dudes that were *hating* on him. I overheard him several times say that these country niggas be *hating* on the "O." The first time he said it I repeated, "The 'O'?"

"Yeah, Helimite. Orlando! Catch up, slow poke!"

The voice in my head screamed *I can't believe you didn't know what "The O" stood for, Helimite.*

I snapped back to the present and said, "All I know, Cartoon, is that *respect* is due to a dog. So, if these cats decided not to give me the *respect*

I'm due, I'll take my *respect* and I promise you they're gonna *hate* the consequences."

Cartoon replied, "Helimite, there's only about eight of y'all at this prison from Palm Beach."

"Yeah, I realize that Cartoon but I'm not talking about the eight. I'm talking about the one. The real one! Helimite! Dorothy Mae Jones' baby boy."

"Helimite, you be serving that fire ass weed around here. And the majority of these dudes wanna get high and don't wanna burn their bridge with you."

"Don't blame it on the weed, Cartoon. Real recognize real no matter where you're at," I said to him.

He responded, "I hear you, dog."

I went back to my bunk and put on some outside winter clothes, grabbed my radio and headed outside to the rec yard. The cold air and the chicken farm smell hit me like I had walked into a freezer. I was en route to the rec yard thinking and listening to my radio at the same time. I hadn't heard from Beth in the longest time. I wondered what she was doing and who she was dating now. Hopefully it was somebody I didn't know. I *hated* when it's a dude I know. Even though I had to *respect* it, I still didn't have to like it. It's been a while since I called to talk to some of my homeboys. So, as soon as I finish working out with Cartoon, I would head back to the dorm and make some phone calls to get the 411 on what the streets was doing in "Raw-viera."

When I walked in the weight cage, Cartoon had 225 pounds on the squat rack already. I sat my radio down and turned it up because *Let's Chill* by Guy was playing. I did a few simple stretch exercises to loosen up and stepped inside the squat rack. I put the 225 pounds on my shoulders.

Ten sets of lunges.

Ten sets of squats.

Then I sat the weight back on the rack to let Cartoon get his first set of ten in. Once we were done, I left the weight cage and walked a lap around the track to ease the tightness in my legs. As I walked, I was looking at all the different colored leaves on the ground and blowing through the air. In that moment, all by myself, I felt the need to talk to God and pray about all the things that were troubling me.

By the time I finally made it back to my dorm, I was tired, but I felt a whole lot better. I headed to my locker and grabbed my phone book. The call I made was to my boy Wee Wee. There was no answer, so I called Sam. He picked up the second ring, accepted the call and said, "Heli! Wassup boy? You alright in there?"

"Yeah, Sam. I'm holdin' it down man."

"They still talking about you out here in these streets, Helimite."

I perked up and said, "For real? What they sayin,' Sam?"

He responded, "You know these girls gon' talk and they still talking about how good your head was in the 80's man."

We both burst out laughing and I said, "Sam, you full of shit and you the biggest freak I know. You was dating them white girls in the 9th grade so you got turned out early, Sam."

"Helimite, you must think I forgot about what you got caught doing at Lincoln Elementary in the 5th grade."

I thought about what he said and couldn't recall what he might be referring to, so I said, "What you talkin' 'bout, Sam?"

"When you got caught with a mirror on the top of your shoes trying to look up under the teacher, Ms. Sanders' dress."

All I could do was laugh. "Sam, you don't forget shit. Ms. Sanders was shocked to know I was that freaky at such a young age."

"Yeah, Heli. When I saw that, I knew you was a bona fide freak, boy."

"I was just curious, Sam."

It was his turn to laugh. We talked for another 15 minutes or so before I hung up. Laughter is so good for the soul. I picked up the phone again to dial my sister Teresa's number. She answered and accepted charges. Me and my li'l sister Teresa, who is actually my big sister because she's older than me, been through a lot growing up together. For years, it was just mama, her, and me. Our bond was deep, at least I felt it was.

She brought me up to speed on all the family affairs and advised me not to send any more money to her address because, "Ain't that much poker-playing going on inside that prison." I had to tell Teresa all that money I sent home was from gambling otherwise it would have been a no-go. Either way, she was stopping it now. I probably shouldn't have called her 'till after new year.

She did tell me mama had mentioned visiting me on Christmas but had to get her car tuned up first. That was good news. Christmas was about eight days away, so I had to get my visiting park clothes washed and pressed. I can't go out there looking any kind of way. If mama didn't teach me nothing else, she taught me to always look like I'm somebody's child.

CHAPTER 28

My homeboy Mater Head was a midget in my eyes. He stood at about four feet and some change, but he was a hustling ass midget. I had him serving weed and running a store. I never had any issue with him about anything until three days before Christmas. He got robbed down in the basement where the pool tables were in the indoor rec building. He came into the dorm all jacked up, huffing and puffing. His buttons were all popped off his jacket and he was looking all wide-eyed, talking loud, and said, "Homeboy! Homeboy! Strap up! Strap up! Them coward ass negros jumped me and robbed me for twelve dimes in the pool room."

I sat up in my bed and said, "Who?"

"Them cats from Tallahassee and Pensacola."

"How they know you had weed on you?" I asked.

He responded, "Because I had just sold a dime bag to one of their homeboys and they circled back on me and yoked me out ten minutes later."

Beach Boy was on the bottom bunk laying there just listening as I was. Mater Head started clapping his hands saying, "Strap up. We gotta handle this shit, Helimite."

I'm sitting there thinking about and processing all that Mater Head had just revealed. I told him, "Calm down and chill. We gon' circle back on them dudes later. Let them smoke and think everything is all good for right now."

Mater Head looked at me and screamed, "What?"

"We can handle that at a later date. They already strapped and expecting for somebody to come running back their way."

Mater Head looked at me and said, "Nigga, you a pussy! And you might as well be fuckin.'"

All the hair on my body stood up. Beach Boy sat up in his bunk and I jumped off mines. Mater Head took about four steps back and pulled up his shirt to reveal that he already had a knife on him.

I told him, "You should have had that knife on you when you was getting robbed, but you didn't, so now that you do have it, your heart is big as an elephant. Get from around my bunk, Mater Head before I make you kill me."

He backed away, talking shit. Beach Boy looked at me and said, "Helimite, I know that's your homeboy but you gonna let him slide with all that disrespect?"

I fired up a joint and responded, "Hell yeah. I got a date coming up with my favorite girl this weekend."

Beach Boy said, "Your girlfriend coming to see you?"

I shook my head from side to side while passing him the joint at the same time and said, "Nope. My mama – Dorothy Mae Jones coming for Christmas, which is three days away and I ain't missing that for nothing in the world."

He started coughing and said, "I feel ya, dog." And passed me the joint back.

I told him, "Fire up a Black & Mild to kill this weed smell."

I climbed back on my bunk, got under the covers, and watched the movement. I began to pray,

> *Lord you know I'm really stupid and just trying to stay humble, trying to treat people the way I want to be treated. I rebuke Satan and his assignment against me. In Jesus name, I pray. Amen.*

I put on my headphones and hit the on button on my radio and listened to *Regulators* by Warren G.

======

Christmas morning was no different than any other morning inside prison. It was all routine, a never-ending cycle. You need to be strong in your mind and your thought process to realize that prison doesn't define you. Prison doesn't have to ruin the rest of your natural life. It can be a setback or a rehabilitation period for you to gather yourself. It all depends on how you apply prison time to your situation. Me, myself, and I had no interest in becoming institutionalized, so I always went against the grain to a certain extent.

I woke up Christmas morning and thanked the Lord for allowing me to see another day and went and took a hot shower. I dried off and proceeded to lotion up my body. I was in my boxer shorts and shower slides. I looked toward the officer's station and could see we had two female officers working our dorm on Christmas. That was rare and indeed a gift to G and H dorm.

I hurry up and put on a t-shirt before the female officers feel like I'm flexing. I lifted my mattress and pulled out my visiting park clothes from between two pieces of cardboard. I had been sleeping on top of my visiting park clothes to keep the creases in my pants and shirt in place. I began to dress and once I finished, I reached in my locker and pulled out a nasal spray bottle and sprayed three squirts of *Aramis* cologne I bought from a dude who got sent back to prison from the work release center. So, not only was I looking like somebody's child, but I was smelling like one too.

I really wanted to smoke one, but I decided against it. I needed to be in my right mind talking to my mama. An hour passed and finally the intercom came to life, "Inmate Helimite, report to the visiting park."

I walked up to the officer's station, showed my I.D. so Officer Bell could write me a pass to get me through the center gate check point. She wrote me a pass then handed it to me and said, "You smell good, Helimite."

"Thank you, Ms. Bell."

She responded, "When they started selling cologne in a canteen?"

I looked at her and shrugged my shoulders and walked toward the exit door. I walked out with a lot of pep in my step. I got to the visiting park shake down room and got searched from head to toe. They didn't make me strip down, which was alright with me. I walked through the door looking from left to right for my mama.

The visiting park was packed from the front to back, wall to wall, but my mama had gotten here early enough to secure a table that would sit four people easy. She had food and a monopoly game board on the table. We probably wouldn't play it but it was there to occupy the extra space at the table so no one would ask to sit with us.

I hugged my mama and said, "I love you ma. Merry Christmas.

Thanks for coming. It's so good to see you."

"It's good to see you too, son. You look good. I see you still lifting weights and puttin' on weight."

"Yes, ma'am. I gotta stay fit, mama. It's a lot of foolishness going on in there. As you would always say, mama, the devil stay busy."

"I know that's right, son."

My mama had a blue t-shirt on that said, "I trust God." And, that, she did! We began to talk about some of everything. My sisters Teresa, Tanya, Tamia and Keyna were at home in West Palm Beach. All doing well.

"Thank the Lord," she said. As I looked around the visiting park to see where the microwave was to heat up my sandwich, I noticed that me and mama was the only black people on the visiting park. No, wait a minute. There's one black lady standing up against the wall waiting patiently for someone to come inside. My mama spotted her as well, and said, "Go tell that sister we have room at our table for her."

I get up from the table to do as my mama had asked. I approached the sister and repeated what my mama had said. She said, "Thank you," and headed to our table.

I went to the microwave and waited my turn in line to heat up my food. I looked over the visiting park and saw Kearns from Ohio at a table in the corner with a nice-looking girl in deep conversation. He must have felt me looking because he looked up at me and gave me a head nod.

When I walked back to the table, my mama and the other lady was talking like they had been knowing each other for years. I sat down and started eating my sandwich. They continued to talk about God and their kids. She mentioned she had traveled a good ways to see her baby boy. I kept eating and a few minutes later her baby boy had finally showed up.

The first words out of his mouth was, "Mama. You should have told me you was coming. I would have been already dressed and waiting."

I looked up and said, "You probably had to do a hundred pushups before you came out here."

"Yeah, I did a hundred. And you must have done 200 as tight as that shirt is."

The whole table laughed.

"Y'all know each other?" my mama asked.

"Yes, ma'am. That's one of my students," Cartoon said.

"One of your students?" my mama repeated.

Before Cartoon could answer, I said, "He is my tutor in the education department here. I'm in the process of taking my GED test and Carlton passed it awhile back and became a teacher's aide."

My mama was impressed and said, "Praise God. Bless your soul, young man."

"And he's my student inside the weight cage. We work out together, ma," I responded.

"Everything happens for a reason," my mother said. She turned to Cartoon's mom and asked, "Where did you say y'all was from again, Stephanie?"

"Orlando."

My mother said, "We're from Riviera Beach and I'm so glad to hear that our young men are making good use of their time in here.

Ms. Stephanie said, "To God be the glory. Yes, because y'all not gonna be in here forever. God has a plan for both of y'all. Just be ready and willing for him to use you even inside this prison."

I'm shaking my head, side to side. "Mama, they crazy and out of control at this prison. Am I lying, Carlton?"

He gave me the sideways look for calling him Carlton for the second time. What could he say, his mama named him that, right? He just responded, "Yep they be trippin' out there."

We talked some more about how the prison was being ran. Then me and my mama went to take a few pictures. I grabbed a domino set off the game table and took it back to our table where Cartoon and his mama were eating and talking. We sat back down, and I asked Ms. Stephanie if she wanted to play some dominoes with us when they were through eating.

She replied, "Yes," and ten minutes later our table was wide open with laughter and competition with the dominoes. Cartoon kept telling me to knock on wood "…because I know you can't play on that five down there." I *hated* when he was right, but I *respectfully* had to knock on wood so they could pass me.

We were having a wonderful time despite being inside of a prison. The sergeant over the visiting park announced, "15 minutes till this visiting park closes." Hearing that announcement always made me sad. We began to put the dominoes up and say our goodbyes. My mama said, "Wait a minute. I almost forgot." She reached in her pocket and pulled out her prayer oil.

I asked, "Mama. Security let you bring your prayer oil in?"

She responded, "Yes. They asked what it was, and I told them. They looked kinda scared like I might be the root lady or something, but God is always opening doors and prison gates as well." She opened the bottle, put prayer oil on my head and Cartoon's head and we all joined hands.

Mama began to pray over me and Cartoon asking God, "To shield and protect us, cover us at all times, and to order our steps through this prison journey. Lord, we thank you for what you're doing and what you will be doing for their lives in the future. I rebuke Satan's assignment against our sons in Jesus' name. Amen."

Me and Cartoon both had a shiny forehead from the cross mama had put there with the prayer oil. Ms. Stephanie gave me a hug and whispered in my ear and said, "Look after your other brother."

I said, "Yes, ma'am. I will."

Cartoon hugged my mama. I hugged and kissed my mama on her cheek and told her I love her and to drive safe over to Georgia to granny's house.

CHAPTER 29

We both left the visiting park in good spirits and arrived back to our dorm to see them same faces we had left five hours ago. Yeah, it was Christmas, but Santa Claus wasn't going to slide our way with any joy and gifts. It was up to you, as an individual, to make Christmas day feel like a holiday. So, I always had a party or gathering with my circle of friends and today was no different. I had ordered three loafs of bread, a big ass can of tuna, mayo, mustard, onions, tomatoes, and twelve boiled eggs.

I told Cartoon to come over to my bunk in an hour. He agreed and went and got on the phone. I gave Hustleman, who worked in the kitchen, $40 dollars in weed to bring me all the ingredients I needed to make my chain gang famous tuna salad. I didn't have a bowl to mix all this tuna up, so we cleaned out a three-gallon bucket from the kitchen that used to be filled with chicken base.

I changed out of my visiting clothes and put them back underneath my mattress, turned my radio on, and listened to Kurtis Blow Christmas rappin', while I opened this huge can of tuna stolen from the kitchen. This one can would feed eight to ten people, easy.

Cartoon walked up and said, "Helimite, you finna throw down on the grocery."

I nodded my head up and down and said, "Yeah. Sit back and take notes. I don't give out my tuna recipe to just anybody, so consider your country ass privileged right now."

"Country," he screamed and laughed. "Helimite, you still wearing Converse tennis shoes. You stuck in the 80's dude. It's all about Jordans now."

I told Cartoon, "These Converse cost way more than them Jordan's you got on."

Cartoon started laughing again and said, "That's the same reason why you need to stop smoking that stank ass weed. It's killing your brain cells."

"I'm glad you said that, Cartoon." I looked over at Beach Boy and said, "Roll one up soul brother," as I continued to make up the tuna salad. I had three brand new razors to cut up the tomatoes and onion with it. I had the whole back of the dorm smelling like a restaurant.

Somebody yelled out, "One time," meaning the C.O. was walking around inside the dorm. It was Officer Bell. She was smelling good and looking good. Her hair was done in a finger wave style, lip gloss on. Fingernails painted light blue to match her contact lenses. I kept on mixing up my tuna salad when she got to my bunk and saw what I was doing.

She said, "Well, damn. Y'all 'bout to have a party and wasn't gonna invite me."

I said, "Ms. Bell, you the boss lady. You don't need an invite. Once I'm done, I'll bring you a sandwich and a bag of chips and an ice-cold coke or sprite to wash it all down."

She looked at me and said, "Make that two. Officer Wooden is gonna want something to eat as well and I'm not sharing mine."

"I gotcha, Ms. Bell," and she kept it moving.

Cartoon waited till she was far enough away to make his next comment. "Your country ass swear you got game for the ladies."

I looked at Cartoon while I crushed up the bag of bbq corn chips to add to the bucket and said, "I'm undefeated with the ladies and with these hands."

Cartoon snapped back, "From what I heard, you ain't thrown no hands yet. You undefeated with that pipe you been using to hit people with."

I laughed and said, "Cartoon, ain't no rules in fighting. A win is a win and why mess my knuckles up when I don't have to? If anybody try me somewhere on the compound where I can't get to my pipe, I will lay hands on them and it won't be for prayer, by the way. You still have that shining cross on your forehead that my mama put up there."

He touched it and rubbed it into his forehead. "So, you a preacher's son?"

"Yeah, Cartoon. My mama is a pastor and my daddy is a straight concrete-laying-cocaine-selling-boss-player." I began telling him stories about my daddy. I removed the plastic gloves I had been cooking with and threw them away. I pulled out all three of my photo albums and gave them to Cartoon to look through. Beach Boy fired that blunt up and when he did, Cartoon covered his nose with his shirt while flipping through the photo albums. He stopped and got stuck on a picture of Nicole and asked me, "Who is this?"

I told him, "Don't-Get-Your-Jaw-Broke-Nicole." We all burst into laughter.

He then said, "You like them red girls."

I said, "Believe it or not, they like me. Red and black go together."

I passed the joint back to Beach Boy, pulled out a loaf of bread and made two tuna salad sandwiches, wrapped them up in napkins, along with two bags of regular Lays chips and placed them on my top bunk. I pulled out two cans of soda from a five-gallon bucket with sodas and ice in it and took them to the officer's station. I handed everything to Officer Bell and said, "Merry Christmas, Ms. Bell and Ms. Wooden."

She took the food and handed Ms. Wooden half of what I gave her.

Ms. Wooden said, "Ain't nothing in here gonna make me sick?"

"I doubt it. I would never do anything like that. You somebody child, somebody mama, somebody sister or aunt. You need me to take a bite out of your sandwich first?" I asked.

"No. I was just teasing. Officer Bell told me you was down there with food service gloves on. If you went that far to have gloves on while preparing the food, you cooking clean. And it doesn't hurt that you stay clean and be smelling good."

Ms. Bell added, "You different, Helimite." She asked me, "Who came to visit you today? Your girlfriend?"

"Naw. My mother dropped in on me."

"Nice," Ms. Bell said. "Did you enjoy your visit?"

"Absolutely! Imma go eat, ladies. When I'm done, I'll come back and kick it with y'all as long as Sgt. McMillian crazy ass don't show up."

"I know thas right," Officer Wooden said.

And I turned to head back to my bunk. I get there and tell Cartoon,

"You still in Palm Beach County looking my homegirls over?"

He closed the one photo album he was looking at and said, "Yeah but it's chow time now."

"Yes, it is. Fix you a sandwich. Chips in that locker over there and the sodas are in the bucket behind that laundry bag in the corner."

We both fixed sandwiches and sat down to eat and talk. He asked me if I was ready for the upcoming GED test. I told him that I was but that I probably wouldn't be here to take it. He looked at me curiously and said, "You headed back to court or something?"

I said, "No. I gotta handle some shit right here on the compound and I may end up in confinement or get transferred. **Quiet As Kept**. I was just holding off on it until I got to see my mama."

"What's going on? You know your mama hugged me and told me to keep you under my wings, so you don't get hurt inside here."

"Yeah. Imagine that Cartoon. My mama know I'm a fool when I need to be. A few cats from up north, Pensacola, robbed Mater Head a while back so I gotta touch them up and Mater Head for disrespecting me."

"What did he do?"

"He told me that I was a pussy and I need to be fuckin,' because I refused to step down on the dudes that robbed him that same day."

His eyes widened and then he said, "You bullshittin'."

"Nope. That's what he said. Beach Boy was right here when he said it. I let it ride because I wasn't gonna miss my visit with my mama but it's on now."

Before I could say another word, the dorm P.A. system came on, "Attention in the dorm. Attention in the dorm. All inmates report to your bunks for count. You have five minutes before count time." Cartoon fixed another sandwich and went to his bunk.

CHAPTER 30

Christmas day came and went. I was so full off them tuna sandwiches that I went to sleep before midnight. I gave away the rest of the tuna to my circle of people who slept around me in this open dorm. I was in the process of putting my plan together on the unfinished business I had to tend to. I was already informed that Mater Head was carrying his knife 24-7 now, so I had to catch him without it to ensure he didn't stick me. I knew just what I had to do to achieve that. All I had to do was lay and wait and I was the best in the world at doing that.

It was December 26, 1994. It was still considered a holiday inside the prison. A lot of staff didn't show up for work that day, which was good for what I had in mind. I went to the recreation yard and did 500 jumping jacks and 100 toe touches. Cartoon was on the basketball court doing his thang and talking shit at the same time. When he finished, he came to the outfield of the softball field to mess with me. The first thing he said was, "I think I like your homegirl, Niecy. She my type."

I shook my head and said, "Cartoon, Niecy is way too much for you, but I'm gonna call her tonight and put your scary ass on the phone with her. It's up to you to get her address and number while you're on the phone with her."

Cartoon responded, "That's a bet, Helimite. I'm from the Ivey Lane projects in Orlando, Florida. She can't do nothing but tell me, 'No,' and 'no' has never stopped me before, but I doubt she will after listening to me. I can talk a cat off a fish truck if the cat listens."

"Alright, Cartoon. We will see. I'm going back to the dorm to shower up and lay down." I gave him a fist bump and left the rec yard.

Beach Boy was always somewhere nearby with knives on him. When I arrived in the dorm, I noticed Mater Head wasn't on his bunk or in the TV room. I checked the bathroom, and he wasn't there either, so I walked by the showers and glanced in there and there he was, lathered all up with soap in his eyes trying to get clean. He wasn't the only person in there, but it didn't matter. I had the opportunity I was looking for.

I walked right into the shower with my shorts and boots on and punched Mater Head in his rib cage with all my might. He never saw it coming. He grunted like a wild pig as he buckled and hit the shower floor. I kicked him twice in the stomach and then went to his clothes, found the knife he had been carrying and put it inside my waist band. I looked at him on the ground squealing like a pig. The other guy who was in the shower vanished as soon as he saw me throw the first blow. I looked down at Mater Head and said, "Now, you look like you ready to be somebody bitch."

I walked back and gave the knife to Beach Boy and said, "Add it to your collection, Dog."

I sat on my bunk, facing the shower and watching Mater Head struggle to get off that nasty ass shower room floor. Once he was able to stand up, with the assistance of the shower wall, he screamed out to another inmate, "Hey. Go tell the Police. It's a medical emergency in the shower area and I need a wheelchair ASAP!"

I watched the inmate run to the officer's station and relay Mater Head's message. The young, black C.O. shot out of the officer's station like it was on fire while he pushed that new emergency panic button at the same time.

I looked down at Beach Boy on his bunk and said, "If I go to confinement, send me three packs of cigarettes and at least ten Snicker bars every week." Beach Boy already knew what inmates were holding food and smokes in their lockers for me. "If they transfer me, Beach Boy. Keep all that stuff and keep it flippin' and live off the interest, dog."

He nodded his head in agreement and asked, "You think your homeboy gonna tell them white folks on you fo' real?"

I looked at Beach Boy and said, "I never imagined that he would disrespect me like that after all I have done to make his situation better but, at this point, I don't put nothing past that nigga."

About eight officers and two nurses showed up at G dorm with a wheelchair. I could hear Sergeant McMillan's big stupid ass keep asking Mater Head what happened. And I could clearly hear Mater Head say, "I slipped and fell in the shower, sarge. I think I broke something." I could hear Mater Head scream out, "Owwwww!!!" He moaned as he was guided into the wheelchair.

I looked toward the front door when it slammed shut and Cartoon was walking toward my bunk with a look of curiosity on his face. "What happened to Mater Head, Helimite?"

"Well, from what I just heard, Carlton, he fell in the shower," I answered.

Cartoon looked at me sideways and said, "The only two people that can call me Carlton is my mama, Stephanie and my pops, Wayne. Your country ass call me Carlton again, you gon' fall in the shower next."

"If you ain't gonna kill me, Carlton, just leave it alone plus you don't weigh enough to be bumpin' with me li'l brother. I'm gonna test that 210 pounds out that you say you weigh."

"I just gotta catch you without that pipe around, Helimite."

"I know thas right O-town."

We both laughed. I got off my bunk once all the officers and nurses left. I pulled my phone book out and told Cartoon, "I'm 'bout to call Niecy now so bring your square ass on."

"Watch your mouth, Helimite, before I break your jaw and have you eating out a straw."

"Whatever, man."

I picked up the phone and dialed Niecy's number. She picked up on the third ring. I asked her how she was doing and how her family was doing. She said that all was well, and it was so good to hear from me. It had been at least a year since I called her, and she insisted that I call more. Niecy was my homegirl from the back of Stoneybrook. My soul brother Vell used to date her, so we had never been anything but friends. What I loved about her was that she always wrote me and sent pictures, and pictures were worth a thousand words in prison. Seeing is believing.

"So, Niecy," I said, in my most relaxed tone of voice. "I have a partner who's from Orlando who couldn't stop looking at your pictures in my photo album. He a solid dude, Niecy, and he wants to put a voice with the pictures he been lookin' at."

"You say he solid, Helimite. You can put him on the phone."

I turned to my right and handed Cartoon the phone and walked away, climbed back in my bed and turned my radio back on. The sounds of Tevin Campbell was playing. *I'm Ready*. The song was playing, and I was thinking that *I'm ready too* but not for love. I'm ready to get some payback. The cats who robbed Mater Head knew Mater Head wasn't the source. They knew he was just a worker.

In this razor wire confined world that I'm stuck in for the moment, it's a must that I address this with violence, of course. It's the only option that will be **respected** and understood. They started this with violence, plus I'm pretty sure the clock is ticking for those cats to try and roll up on me thinking I'm soft.

You know the old saying, "Give somebody an inch, their next move is coming for a yard." As much as I tried to always be a pure player, it just doesn't work out like that in the prison system. These fools see me with the pressed clothes, the jewelry, and of course they smell the cologne. They size me up every time as being on the humble and soft side of things, but what can I say? I'm in my lane and I'm not changing lanes for nobody.

I raised up from my bunk, looked down at Beach Boy and asked, "Did them white boys from the maintenance shop deliver that pipe yet?"

He smiled and said, "Hell yeah. It's a nice one, Helimite. I got it inside the mattress on bunk 97. The locker broke on that bunk so they can't assign nobody to it 'til it get fixed."

I nod my head up and down, "I'm gonna need it tomorrow, man. So, dig it back out when everybody leave for breakfast in the morning."

Beach Boy responded, "I gotcha, dog."

I hopped down from my bunk, pulled out a deck of cards from out my locker. I get Malik, Bump City, and Beach Boy to sit down for a game of spades. This was also my best time to explain to all three of them what I planned to do the next day and what I needed them to do for me while it all went down. It was simple. Watch and protect my back and handle any would-be heroes, homeboys, sightseers, and the crowd that might gather. All three nodded in agreement.

I looked at Malik and Bump City and said, "If y'all need some fire or extra fire, let Beach Boy know."

Bump City looked at me and said, "Come on, Helimite. You know I keep it on me."

Malik laughed and said, "Me Too. I'm the only cat here from Louisiana. I don't never know what y'all Florida boys be thinking or what y'all be up to."

I glared at Malik. "You 6'8", 240. Ain't nobody from Florida or anywhere else just trying to pick a fight with you. At this prison, you straight, dog."

"You just never know, Helimite," he responded.

"At the end of the day, you dead right, Malik."

Cartoon walked up to our card game and said, "Helimite, you play chess?"

I looked up at Cartoon and said, "Naw. I'm not that smart, Cartoon, to be playing chess. I play checkers. Too much thinking gives me a headache. Why you think I don't have my GED yet?"

Everybody laughed.

I looked back at Cartoon and asked, "You straight?"

He answered, "Ivey Lane always straight. Believe that."

Cartoon behind the razor wire (1993)

CHAPTER 31

"Girl, keep that pussy right there and don't move," I repeated for the third time even though I knew she wouldn't cooperate. As I proceeded to walk that dick back up inside of her, moving her soft ass cheeks apart to drive myself deeper into her soul, she moaned and pushed her body back against mine and whispered, "Fuck me, Helimite."

"Shhhh. Be quiet and let me work," I said as I moved my hands to her lower back. I pinned her down so she couldn't move again and began to pound away inside of her. Dr. White took her thumb and put it in her mouth and began to shiver and moan and let her juices flow as I provided her with the dick down she wanted. And she provided me with the pussy I needed since I didn't get a chance to bust a nut last time we fucked. She messed that up when she decided to piss on me, but today would be different.

I looked down at my dick rhythmically going in and out of her. Her ass was so perfectly round and flawless. Me watching our movements of lust would prove to be my mistake as the sight of me giving it to her overwhelmed my sense of pleasure and I could no longer hold back. I pulled Dr. White to me and held her tight and released my seed deep inside of her as she called my name.

And then the lights came on. "G-Dorm, get ready for breakfast," the officer stated over the P.A. system. I lay there looking up at the yellow stained ceiling and knew it was all a dream, but a wet dream for sure. Sperm was all over my thigh and boxer shorts. Dr. White had me really feenin' for her.

I couldn't go to breakfast, so I lay there and waited 'til the dorm left for the chow hall and for the lights to go back off. It was 5:30 in the morning and the dorm still smelled like smoke. All I could hear was snoring and that squeaky ceiling fan. I sat up and said my routine morning prayer. I propped my pillow up some more and looked over the dorm once again before going to the bathroom area. I needed to wash myself off in the sink since the shower was off limits until the shift changed.

I *hated* open bay dorms. All these bunks piled in on top of each other, barely any walking space. I looked to my left once again and what I was seeing now was like a scene out of an army training film. This was prison, not the military yet someone was sliding on their stomach and elbows in between the bunks like a Navy Seal. I don't know where he was going or coming from, but I'm pretty sure he had a knife on him. It could be a booty bandit going to take some ass or a paid hitman. I don't know. It wasn't my business. It be so much going on behind the scenes in these prisons. People in society be thinking that prison guards' control, see, and protect us from all harm and danger. These TV shows about prison life have them fooled.

I couldn't see the Navy Seal. He was last seen headed in the direction opposite from me. So, I eased myself off that top bunk, opened my locker, get my toothbrush and toothpaste, soap, and a pair of clean boxer shorts. On my way to the bathroom, I stopped dead in my tracks and turned around to get my washcloth and towel. I was trying to hurry up before my dorm comes back from breakfast. I don't need anyone seeing me butt naked, taking a bird bath in the bathroom sink area.

After washing up, I returned to my bunk to put on some cold weather clothing. It was cold outside, and I had to layer up to keep that 30-degree wind chill off me. To my surprise, Beach Boy was awake and was blowing his nose and complaining about his sinuses acting up. He looked at me and said, "Whassup," and then pulled the blanket back on his bed to reveal the pipe I had ordered.

I turned my back to the officer's station, picked up the pipe and sized it up against my wrist to my shoulder. "With my 2X prison coat on, it will fit perfectly, dog." I handed the pipe back to Beach Boy and tell him that I will get it once the rec yard opens.

Breakfast was coffee cake, oatmeal, and an apple, but my dorm still wasn't back yet, which tells me the kitchen must have run out of something.

I walked to the back of the dorm and looked out the window. I couldn't see anything outside because it was still too dark outside. I could hear the wind whistling. I gotta find a way to get to a prison in south Florida. The panhandle was not a good fit for me.

I walked back to my bunk and got back under the covers. I must have dozed off because I never heard my dorm return from the kitchen. Because it was a Saturday, the officers wouldn't do their regular routine for count. Meaning, nobody would have to sit in an upright position for count. The more people that stayed asleep meant less work that the officers would have to deal with.

The rec yard opened around 8:45 a.m. I suited up with all my cold weather gear, slid my pipe up my right sleeve, and grabbed my Super 2 Radio and headed out the door. The wind was blowing like crazy, but today was the first time I didn't smell that stank ass chicken farm.

The rec yard was just like any hood on the street. It was very territorial. Every hometown clique and gang affiliation had a certain section of the rec yard that they held down. Every day, like a drug corner, them Tallahassee boys and Pensacola cats rolled together under the same pavilion over by the softball field. They stayed ten to twenty deep over there playing cards and dominos. I was way outnumbered, but I had the element of surprise on my side.

I looked like I was just outside for a morning walk with my radio in hand jamming Craig Mack, *Brand New Flava In Ya Ear*! Beach Boy, Malik, and Bump City all arrived at separate times to the rec yard. There was hardly anyone outside. It was just too cold and too early, I guess. The section them Tallahassee and Pensacola boys held down was a ghost town. I tell my guys that we will circle back around after lunch.

Since I had the whole morning to spare, I decided to stop by the kitchen and place an order with Hustleman on a few things I needed. I was at the Dining Hall side window. It helped block me from the wind. I could smell that nasty ass liver they were already throwing on the grill for lunch. I hollered through the broken window to one of the guys cleaning the dining room to get Hustleman for me. A few minutes later Hustleman finally appeared.

Hustleman was from Louisiana and relocated to Florida and ended up catching a case. Here he was, 6'3", blacker than the boots I had on and always had a dirty kitchen apron on like he was official business, always hard at work. He reminded me of Richard Pryor because he was always clowning and full of jokes. As I was placing my order, he spotted Officer Bell walking down the sidewalk. "Helimite," he said. "Officer Bell sholl got something to shit with."

I looked to my right and seen Officer Bell walking that walk, heading over to G and H dorm. I responded, "Yeah, Hustleman. She fine as can be, bro."

He answered back, "Yeah. If she was my woman, we wouldn't need any toilet paper in the house."

I looked up at him through the broken window with a look of curiosity on my face and said, "What are you sayin', man?"

He responded, "Dog, I'm not trippin,' but I'll eat and blow all up in her ass 'til her nose runs."

I busted into laughter while shaking my head from left to right. "Hustleman, you been locked up way too long. My appetite don't call for all that but whatever turns your big freaky black ass on, bro."

I changed the subject back to the business we were conducting and asked him if he could deliver my order today. He agreed and I turned and left the kitchen and walked to the canteen. I bought two jungle juices and some salted peanuts before I headed back to the dorm to get out of the cold for a minute. I also needed Beach Boy to slide over with me to the library to check out at least twelve National Geographic magazines. That was my go-to magazine to take me from the prison and into far away countries and places I have never been before. It relieved my mind from the programmed routine of prison life. It could be a life saver when things got situational as well.

It was getting close to noon count. I climbed back up on my top bunk and took off a layer of winter clothes since the heater in the dorms was actually working. I turned on my radio, put my headphones on and listened to Janet Jackson sing about *Control*. I guess control is something everybody seeks, for different reasons, of course. Control over your finances. Control over an addiction. Control over him or her. You just never know. All I wanted was control back over my life again. The Florida Department of Corrections had control and the last say so on what went on with me.

I took a deep breath and told myself, *this too shall pass*. I really wanted to fire up a joint, but it was too close to count time. I lay there and let the music consume me. I had received quite a few Christmas cards that I needed to send thank you letters back. Hazellee, Octavia, Barbette, and Tasha all thought about me over the holiday, and I was grateful that they thought about me. I actually have enough stamps and envelopes to reach out to everyone in my address book. I don't know what all I could possibly say to all them folks after all the years that have passed. It had been at least seven months since I talked to Beth. I doubt I can heal whatever hurt or pain I may have caused her, but hopefully she understood I was hurting and angry when I said all that I said. And then there was Nicole Ventress. What started out as a crush in the 5th grade in Mr. Walker's classroom at Lincoln Elementary had finally materialized into a relationship in high school.

From the moment I saw her after the four years since Mr. Walker's classroom, I had to have her. I was at Twin Lakes High School Homecoming, and there she was rolled out on a float as the homecoming queen. I applied myself and seized the moment only to see it all end a few short months later due to me deciding to go to prison for 55 years. What was I thinking? I'm pretty sure I won the Silly-Negro-of-the-Year award in 1987 for that decision.

My mama keeps saying that this is only a test, and that God has so much more in store for me. There's no class on how to do 55 years in prison, so it's like on-the-job training, survival for me. I just gotta keep waking up as I watch the years go by.

When Hustleman enters the dorm, you will know it. He always shouts out what he has. "Ain't no deals. All money on the wood." Today was no different. He had liver sandwiches with cheese and fried potato logs for a pack of cigarettes, which was around three dollars at the time. He had already sold out by the time he reached the back of the dorm to my bunk. Hustleman reached into his jacket and handed me a large roll of saran wrap. I asked him, "What I owe you, Hustle?" He wanted a bag of mud a.k.a. coffee. I paid him and he kept it moving.

Count time came and left. It was still cold outside but had warmed up some due to the sun showing its face. I looked out the window at the chow line that was steady growing for that liver and onions with mashed potatoes and mixed vegetables. The best thing about being able to afford to miss this meal or any other meal affords me a little one-on-one time to conversate with whoever the dorm officer might be for the day. For G-dorm, it just so happened to be Officer Bell's fine ass again.

I eased up to the officer's station to speak to her. "Good afternoon, Ms. Bell."

She looked up from her officer's logbook and said, "Hello, Helimite. Why you didn't go eat?"

"I'm allergic to liver, Ms. Bell. So, I'll be having a peanut butter and honey sandwich for lunch."

She stared up at me with a curious look on her face. "That's it? That's all you eating?"

"Yeah," I said, "And a few granola bars and that's it 'til dinner time."

She nodded her head up and down and stated, "Oh, you eating healthy. I need to take a page out of your book. I'm trying to lose twelve pounds."

I looked at her sideways, "Where you trying to lose it at?"

She pointed to her hips and ass. "I can write you up a workout plan if you serious, Ms. Bell. It's a simple three-day workout, but you have to drink at least two gallons of water everyday as well." She stared at me like I was telling her some top-secret stuff, and I'm looking at her like, "Your fine ass need to stop playing."

She stood up and said, "My sister getting married in three months and I need to be able to fit in my dress."

"I'll write up the routine, Ms. Bell. The rest is up to you."

CHAPTER 32

The dorm door opened. A few dudes were returning from eating. One of the dudes pulled up next to me to bother Officer Bell for some Tylenol. I looked back at Officer Bell and continued, "I'll circle back." I walked back to my bunk and fixed my peanut butter and honey sandwich and washed it down with that last jungle juice.

I grabbed the five-gallon bucket that had ice and sodas in it and took it to the shower area and emptied the water out. Once Beach Boy, Malik and Bump City came back from the kitchen, I called them over to my bunk. I tell them that it seemed like it had warmed up outside so them busters might go to the rec yard after lunch. "Y'all know they be deep over there under the pavilion. We will, clearly, be outnumbered. So, we need to suit all the way up just in case."

Malik and Bump City looked at me all confused. "What you mean, Helimite?"

I tell Beach Boy to grab all the National Geographic magazines. I pulled out the saran wrap I bought from HustleMan and said, "Meet me behind the shower wall."

I had the five-gallon bucket turned upside down to use as a seat. Beach Boy removed his shirt, and I placed a National Geographic magazine on his torso. One in front. One in back and one on each side of his waist going up to his armpit. I ask Malik and Bump City to hold the magazines in place. I put the saran wrap on the front of Beach Boy's stomach and wrap his torso, creating the prison version of a knife-proof vest. Once it was tight and secure, I added a magazine to each forearm and saran wrap it to him. Once I was done, Beach Boy puts on a large gray sweatshirt and gets off the bucket to let whoever was next to sit down. I tell Bump City to take off his shirt and to have a seat and we repeated the same process. Then we did Malik.

40 minutes later, the P.A. system came to life and announced that the yard was open. Like a barn full of cattle being released to graze, all four dorms stampede out trying to get to their favorite game or workout equipment first, so they don't have to wait. The same goes for the basketball court. Whoever gets there first to check out the ball picks four more guys to run with him on the first game. After that, it gets tricky on who the other first five on the court will be, and who had next from that point forward. I *hate* to say it, but if you're not well *respected* as a man or a baller, you could get muscled out. It be a lot going on and around that basketball court and today would prove no different.

I walked out the door toward the backend of the crowd to get downhill to the rec yard. I had my radio in my left hand and was jamming 2pac, *Keep Ya Head Up*. My pipe was tucked away in my right sleeve. Beach Boy, Malik, and Bump City went out ahead of me to get in position and to look everything over. When I reached the basketball court, I noticed one of Cartoon's homeboy, Wayne, arguing with JB from Miami. Wayne wasn't too big in size to be going back and forth with JB who towered over him in height and reach, but Wayne had a big heart. If it came down to throwing hands though, JB's weight and reach had the advantage over Wayne.

I walked behind the basketball bleachers and posted up to watch the movement and outcome of the drama playing out by the court. I turned my head to the left and seen Malik. He nodded, signaling that everybody was on point. I looked back toward the court and heard Cartoon's voice yelling, "You ain't taking my homeboy down, JB, with that gorilla shit. You might as well fight me. He too small for you to be trying to fight, so I'll take the fade for him."

JB looked at Cartoon and said, "Bro, I don't have no beef with you. We good."

Cartoon answered, "If you sizin' up my li'l homeboy Wayne, we can't be good. I'll take the fade, bro."

I was standing at least 20 feet away and heard the entire conversation. I got hot as fish grease that Cartoon had volunteered to fight JB's big

129

Respectfully Hated

ass, so Wayne didn't have to. JB was at least 6'4", 220 pounds, and spent most of his time on the rec yard hitting the punching bag like he might pursue a boxing career once he got out. Fat Cat from Miami walked up to JB and said, "Let me holler at you for a minute," and they walked away.

I made eye contact with Cartoon and waved him over to me. He walked over all wide-eyed and excited. I asked Cartoon, "Why you volunteering to fight JB for Wayne?"

He answered, "JB trying to be a bully right now and it ain't going down like that. Wayne was out here before JB and called next down and I'm running with him on the court next."

I looked around and all the correction officers were watching the softball game, as usual, not knowing or caring what was about to boil over at this end. I looked back toward the court and seen Fat Cat from Miami, Florida making a three-point shot, and a light-skinned brother from up north get the rebound and not give Fat Cat his change. Meaning if you hit a jump shot from anywhere while warming up, you supposed to get the ball passed right back to you until you finally miss. But that didn't happen. So, when the light-skinned brother from up north went to shoot a jump shot, Fat Cat ran toward him as if he were trying to play defense and blocked the shot and drove a forearm right into the dude's chest, wiping him off the court, laying him out ten feet away, flat on his back. The whole basketball court went silent for about five seconds and then all you heard was, "What y'all fuck boys gon' do? Not a damn thing," Fat Cat yelled, not knowing them up north Florida cats had come to the yard strapped and was already pulling out knives.

"Oh shit, Cartoon. It's going down right now. You strapped?"

He looked around at the chaos that had just kicked off and said, "Hell naw. My strap in the dorm."

I started to take off my shoes and socks. "Cartoon, bro, take off your shoes and socks."

He looked at me and said, "I know you said Mike Bell taught you some Taekwondo back at Hardee C.I. but I ain't into all that karate shit."

"Cartoon, take them shoes and socks off!"

He stood there and watched me take all six D-batteries out the back of my radio. I pushed one of my socks into the other sock so that it was double thick and dropped three D-batteries inside of it and tied a knot at the bottom to keep the weight of the batteries locked in at the bottom of the sock. By now, Cartoon was out of his shoes and socks and following my lead. I handed him the other three batteries and watched him repeat what I

130

had done.

I looked around and saw inmates running around everywhere. Some trying to get up the hill to the dorms, others trying to dig up knives they had buried on the rec yard, and some just trying to find a safe place to duck the chaos. You always hear about how a riot started but never how it truly ended.

I suggested to Cartoon, "Bro, let's get back to the dorm. I'm not dying on this rec yard today." I pulled down my blue prison hat as low as it could go on my head to hide my identity. I slid the pipe down my jacket sleeve and into my hand and started making my way back up the hill, which was at least 75 yards away. Blood was being shed from left to right. I looked back to see where Cartoon was, and he had already disappeared into the mayhem. I can't believe this young mutha fucka didn't stick with me, but then I remembered that he was more than capable of fighting his way up the hill with them prison-made nunchaku. He said he wasn't into karate, but he better be Bruce Lee today, swinging them nunchaku back to the dorm.

My head was on a swivel. I saw two correction officers that were watching the softball game on their walkie-talkies and running for their life. The P.A. system came on giving a direct order for all inmates to report back to their assigned dorms with a bull horn sound on repeat. Every time an inmate came in my direction, I waved that pipe like a baton in the hand of a FAMU band leader and bodies moved clean out my way.

I looked to my left and saw Fat Cat, who started all this shit, in a real bad situation. Even though I wasn't from Miami, in this riot, "down south" was from Fort Pierce to Miami, so we was all together on this one. I made my way over to the rec hut where them north Florida boys was trying to stick Fat Cat. There were two of them trying to get to him, but Fat Cat had something in his hands. What? I couldn't see until one of the dudes tried to reach out and cut him. Fat Cat released a hand full of sand to dude's face, enough to blind him giving Fat Cat a clear shot to him with a straight right hand, knocking him out cold. But that wasn't enough to stop the other dude from trying to move in. I slapped the other dude with the pipe across his back and he fell down to one knee, looked back at me coming with the next swing, and took off running.

Fat Cat screamed, "Bet that up, home team."

"Follow me into the rec hut." This was the basement under one of the dorms. It was used as a pool room. I ran down the three stairs, pushed the door open, and it was empty. I grabbed a pool stick and handed it to Fat Cat. He broke the stick in half, keeping the thicker end of the stick as a weapon to fight his way up the hill to where the dorms were on level ground.

I looked over to my right. Some dudes with tshirts covering half their face had a correction officer on the ground kicking and punching him while searching his pockets in between blows.

CHAPTER 33

The P.A. system was still sounding the alarm and repeating, "All inmates return to your dorms immediately."

I wasn't a rookie anymore when it came to riots. So, for the guys that didn't know how important it was to get back inside their dorms before they lock them doors, they would be in a world of trouble once the rapid response team a.k.a. the goon squad showed up with the National Guard behind them. With that thought in mind, I added some pep to my step to get up the hill to G-dorm.

Once I reached the top of the hill, inmates were running around everywhere. Some with their face covered and some not even caring as the violence had not turned down at all. The grunts and screams of inmates being hit with all kinds of objects and stuck with knives, all shapes and sizes. Some beautiful, shiny and new. Others rusty and reddish looking. There were so many inmates bleeding and fighting outside the dorms. It was going to be a process getting through the dormitory doors.

The cries of young black men in pain, bleeding out, crying, and screaming for their mama was so disturbing. I tried to block it all out and stay focused on reaching the dorm. I was maybe 30 feet away and that's when I heard a scream that was different from all the other screams and cries that I had heard thus far. In front of me, behind a row of hedges was another officer down. I swung my pipe from left to right like a magic wand, making my path clear to the dormitory doorway. I heard the scream again and looked more closely to see what officer was being beat down and robbed for all the dirt and disrespect they had been dishing out as a corrections officer. All those inmates they chose to mistreat over the years would be lined up looking to beat they ass for the old and the new.

As I moved close enough to see over them hedges, it wasn't a beat down or a robbery in effect, it was an all-out rape. Three inmates with their faces half covered had Officer Bell's arms held down above her head, another had her legs pinned down, and the last inmate sat on her stomach. Her shirt was ripped wide open. Her chest was moving up and down from the heavy breathing as she continued to wiggle like a fish out of water, trying to break free from the grasp of these three masked inmates. Why did Officer Bell leave the confines of a locked officer station? To come out and assist in, what was now, a full-scale riot – only to be yoked out and pinned down to be raped. The answer to that question, I'll never know.

The one inmate sitting on her stomach was rubbing and feeling on her breasts as she continued to try to break free. He then slapped the right side of Officer Bell's face with so much force that blood and snot flowed down her face. He screamed, "Bitch, be still before I cut your throat. It don't matter to me if you are dead or alive. We gon' fuck you today!"

Officer Bell's face was now turned in my direction from that slap. Tears were flowing like a river from her eyes and there I stood like a little kid feeling some anger and emotions I hadn't felt in God knows how long. I jumped over the hedges and struck the inmate sitting on her stomach across his face, crushing his nose and jawbone, and at the same time knocking him off Officer Bell and into the grass. I didn't care that there were three of them and just me. I was already over the edge now and ready to break more bones if need be.

I yelled out, "The dogs are coming up the hill," while swinging that pipe hysterically. "The dogs are coming up the hill!" I moved toward the last two masked inmates who released Officer Bell and ran in opposite directions. The one I hit in the face was in the wind as well.

"Get up," I bark at Officer Bell. "Get up and get back in the dorm." She struggled to her feet while trying to button her shirt that no longer had buttons on them. "Get in the dorm, Officer Bell!" She gathered herself the best she could and moved in that direction.

I looked to my left and seen Cartoon coming down the breezeway with his homeboy Wayne. Cartoon had given Wayne one of the socks with the three D-size batteries in it. Me and Cartoon locked eyes. I waved my hand to him to hurry up and we both made it inside the dorm a few yards behind Officer Bell, who was clearly traumatized. She forgot to lock the dorm door behind her. She made a beeline into the officer's station and secured the door and broke down completely into deep, heavy-hearted sobs.

The dorm was quiet. Inmates were broken up into different cliques, strapped, and ready for whatever. I began walking down the aisle, headed to my bunk when the front dorm door was kicked in with a loud boom. I turned around immediately to see one of them north Florida dudes running for his life. He was being chased by a dude named Sleepy T from Fort Pierce. There was a card table made of thick wood that was as long as an ole school Cadillac. The north Florida dude ran to one side of the table and kept running around to keep away from Sleepy T. After three laps around the table, Sleepy T was winded and slightly bent over trying to catch his breath.

Someone in the dorm yelled out, "You need to take off running while he tired."

Before this north Florida cat could decide his plans for escape, Sleepy T gathered himself and took a deep breath, sat his knife down on the floor, and pushed the table toward the back wall that was only three feet away, and pinned the dude at the waist against the wall. Sleepy T reached back and down for his weapon and jumped on top of the table and moved toward his prey who was now trapped and helpless.

The north Florida cat threw up his arm to try and block the first swing of the blade but to no avail. I couldn't tell where he took a hit on that swing, but wherever it was caused him to scream out, "I'm sorry man. Don't kill me! Please don't kill me."

Sleepy T slapped him with the blade across the face and flexed, "Stop beggin', bitch. I'm sending you home to your mama."

The guy must have saw death on the way because he wiggled and moved the table back enough to free himself from what was clearly gonna be his last living day on earth. The officer's station was five feet away from this whole scene, but Officer Bell was in such a state of shock, she couldn't or wouldn't be of any help to dude even if she wanted to. The officer's station had a window where they passed out supplies through. It was about the size of two cereal boxes. The dude dove headfirst into that supply window, landed on the floor of the officer's station with blood pouring from his body and onto the floor.

Officer Bell was completely caught off-guard with the inmate getting into this supposed-to-be-secure officer's station. She freaked out and started screaming at the sight of this bloody body, suddenly, on her officer's station floor. She had to still be shook up from the rape attempt, not knowing dude had just saved his own life. Ain't no way Sleepy T's big ass was gonna fit through that supply window to finish dude off.

Sleepy T couldn't believe how dude had just escaped his wrath. I'm sure you have heard the stories of how ordinary human beings become faster, stronger, wiser in a life-or-death situation. A lot of that was on display today. That movie *White Men Can't Jump* was so far from the truth. It was white boys running and jumping all over the place, trying to survive like they were at an N.F.L. combine – all because they didn't want to die during this riot. Prison officials get to be as inhumane as they want to be. They can beat your ass to sleep and blame it on gang violence.

The cries from the officer's station were loud and clear. "I don't wanna die. Call for a doctor, please!"

Officer Bell stood against the wall in complete shock. The whole dorm was silent, looking and listening and smoking cigarettes, back-to-back. Fat Cat burst through the door with half a pool stick still in his grasp, drenched in sweat, looking wild-eyed at all the different cliques of inmates all huddled up together, strapped and waiting for whatever violence that might come their way. Fat Cat yelled out, "Them crackers are coming through the back gate now. At least 100 deep, with dogs."

I could tell something was up because the P.A. system was no longer asking inmates to report to their dorms, and the sound of the alarm system had gone silent. All I could hear was the static from all the walkie talkies the officers were carrying, along with boots, many boots, marching as one.

Our dormitory door flew open again and J.B. wobbled through the door with one hand on the wall to keep his balance and the other hand holding an ice pick. J.B. had knots on his head, cuts on his face, and blood leaking everywhere on him. He looked over the dorm and started yelling, "It ain't over, you country ass mutha fuckas. Whassup!" As he came off the wall, he screamed, "Home Team, stand up!" He walked down the aisle, stopped and looked at Cartoon and said, "Whassup, my nigga. It ain't over," gripping his knife tighter with his veins showing in his neck, looking as though he might turn into the Hulk.

Cartoon looked at J.B. and said, "Bro, give me that knife. It's over with. Go clean yourself up and change clothes before the goon squad comes through that door and flip your ass."

J.B. stood there for a minute. He was deliriously in deep thought then handed the knife to Cartoon and said, "Hide that for me, dog," and stumbled his way toward the bathroom.

Anybody with ears could hear that the boots were on the ground, moving as one, in our direction. On the compound, the National Guard along with the goon squad were here to take the prison back with every weapon at their disposal – dogs, mace, shields, batons. Not only was the riot over, but the joke was also over. At least three helicopters could be heard outside.

In that moment, my common sense kicked in and I took my pipe and threw it as far away from me and my bunk as I possibly could in the direction of the bathrooms. I apparently caused a chain reaction because all the inmates started getting rid of their weapons as well. If you get caught with any kind of weapon on you or around you, it was going to be really ugly for you – an outside charge, a total beat down by the goon squad, and a transfer to another prison to make sure you couldn't get any revenge on the staff that beat your ass.

These officers had total permission to be inhumane at this point. All I could hear were dogs barking, boots on the concrete and lots of walkie talkie chatter. I know this may sound crazy, but more inmates get killed during this phase than the actual riot itself.

CHAPTER 34

And so, it began. Sergeant McMillen, 6'4", around 230 pounds came into G-dorm with at least 30 other officers I had never seen before. They had dogs, shields, and batons. Sergeant McMillen yelled out, "I'm going to tell all you dumb mutha fuckas one time and one time only. Strip down to your boxer shorts and then sit back on your bunks in an upright position."

Once this was done, Sergeant McMillen led the way to every bunk with 30 officers right behind him, dressed in black t-shirts and army fatigue pants and black steel toe boots. He stopped at every single bunk and had every inmate hold out their hands, checking their knuckles for cuts, bruises or swelling. And then he looked over your torso and had you turn around, 360, for him. If he didn't like what he saw, he slapped the shit out of you and had the officers behind him cuff you up and take you to confinement.

Sergeant McMillen was slapping the shit out of inmates and daring them to swing back, calling them, "Coward ass," "Pussy mother fucka," even spitting in their faces. He was eight bunks away from me and Beach Boy. He was at this dude named Zeke's bunk. Zeke had his gay lover sleeping on the top bunk over him. When sarge got to Zeke, he had Zeke doing a 360 turnaround and once his back was turned, sarge slapped him so hard, it sounded like a firecracker had went off.

Zeke screamed out, "You a bitch, sarge. If you was locked up in here with us, I'd fuck your pretty red ass every night with no grease."

Sarge snapped and grabbed Zeke by the throat and drove him to the ground with several other officers following his lead. They was whooping Zeke's ass then all of a sudden Zeke's prison wife couldn't take it no more and he screamed, "Leave my husband alone. He ain't did nothing." As he jumped off his top bunk, he landed on top of Sergeant McMillen's back, scratched him in the face, and started biting into his flesh.

All the officers that were assaulting Zeke went stupid with their batons on the prison wife. Zeke and his prison wife were beaten senseless, and hog tied on the floor, laying in a puddle of their own urine, feces and blood. This situation was beyond crazy, and I cannot lie when I tell you that I was scared as fuck at this point. And I'm sure the rest of G-dorm was as well. The only good that came from this was that Sergeant McMillen was taken out of the dorm to assist with the removal of Zeke and his prison wife – first to Medical then on to confinement.

A white Captain by the name of Zipper took over the examination of each inmate in the dorm. When he got to me, he looked at my face, hands, chest, and back and asked, "Where are you from, inmate?"

"Riviera Beach, Florida, sir," I responded loud and clear.

He looked at the officers to his left and said, "Lock him up under investigation but let him put some clothes on first."

I got dressed and was handcuffed and shackled by three officers and escorted over to Medical and then on to the largest confinement in the Florida Department of Corrections, nicknamed The Gator. It was apparent to me that the prison snitches had already turned in their report on why the riot had started and who was involved. All I could do was pray that the goon squad or the National Guard didn't kill or beat my ass in The Gator. There are no cameras to monitor anybody's behavior in The Gator. In The Gator, your life, health, and strength is always hanging on a string. Real talk!

The Gator was built back in the late 1960s and was designed like a maze. One of the officers escorting me took out some keys and opened the door to the main entrance. From the moment I walked in, all I could hear were steel cell doors slamming, people screaming, and a lot of cursing. The officer's station where I was standing had an old wooden desk with a bunch of paperwork scattered across it, along with a set of walkie talkies sitting on chargers. Up against the wall, there were rows of handcuffs and shackles. The room smelled like pine-sol.

The three officers escorting me ordered me to face the wall while they removed my shackles. They kept the handcuffs on my wrists, behind my back. A few minutes passed and the sergeant over The Gator walked in with Sergeant McMillen. The result of the scuffle with Zeke and his prison wife showed with a long, dark red scratch going across the right side of his face. The sergeant over The Gator asked the officers that escorted me why I was here. One of them answered, "Investigation. That's what Captain Zipper said."

He looked over at me and asked, "Investigation for what? We done had a full-scale riot and he sends an inmate back here for investigation?"

The other officers shrugged their shoulders and one of them said, "We're just following orders, sarge."

It appeared to be a lot of tension in the room, so I stayed quiet. Sergeant McMillen was steady cursing and rubbing his face. He caught me looking at him and yelled, "Punk mutha fucka, what you lookin' at?" He walked over to me, turned me around, and slapped the slob outta my mouth. I never saw it coming. I lost my balance and stumbled a few feet. I held my tongue and anger in check and faced the wall again, but in that moment, I knew I was never going back into open population again.

There was no way I could live here at this prison after being bitch-slapped by Sergeant McMillen. Just like I didn't see that slap coming, Sergeant McMillen wouldn't see my revenge coming as well. ***Quiet As Kept.*** And that's on my mama.

I could hear more inmates entering The Gator. The door squeaked loudly every time it opened. I couldn't see who the inmates were, but I could hear two loud back-to-back slaps. Then I heard Sergeant McMillen laughing and saying, "Y'all mutha fuckas in the Sneads Florida Gatorland now."

The big, cross-eyed sarge, who was the confinement supervisor told the officers that were escorting me to put me in cell D-10. One of the officers grabbed a big, black flashlight off the desk and started moving me in the direction of the cell block. The Gator had enough twists and turns to get you lost. We walked by one cell that was being used as an "understanding room," apparently. Four officers were stomping and kicking somebody's ass to sleep. Whoever it was, crawled under the bottom bunk to get away from the blows. What happened next, I have no idea. I was still being guided by the arm to cell D-10. We turned down a hallway with absolutely no lights. The officer turned on his flashlight and took me about six more steps and pushed me into a cell and slammed the dorm shut.

"Come to the front of the cell," an officer said. He removed the handcuffs off my wrists. He put the flashlight in my face, blinding me, and said, "Welcome to the dark side," and walked away.

The dark side was the worst section of The Gator. The only way you knew what time it was back there was by the meals that came back. If eggs were on the tray, you knew it was breakfast and approximately 6:00 a.m. The cell was hot and smelled like a sour mop had been used. I took off my shirt to cool off some and sat down on the bottom bunk and started to replay all that had unfolded only hours ago. No matter what precautions I took to guard myself from this part of the game, confinement, that is, I still ended up back here.

I was only under investigation, which normally would justify being able to receive most of my property. Investigation was just investigation. The only downfall to that is you could sit back here for 90 days while security acted like they were investigating something. There was so much noise back here with steel doors slamming, radio chatter, inmates going back and forth with officers, and all the hollering and screaming. It was a zoo back here. I was actually glad to be in a cell by myself.

Somebody down the hall kept shaking the cell door screaming, "I want my daddy records. I want my daddy records." What the fuck is this dude talking about, I wondered. Finally, the cross-eyed sergeant walked up to the inmate that was screaming and stated, "Get yo' ass off my door."

The inmate replied in a calm voice, "Sarge, I want my daddy records."

The sergeant answered, "Who the fuck is your daddy?"

"Rick James, bitch!" The inmate burst into loud, hysterical laughter.

"If you shake these bars again," the sergeant started, "I promise you, I'm gonna beat some sense into you. Now get your high yella ass off my door."

I guess dude went and sat down because I didn't hear anything else from him. About two hours had gone by. I was laying down on a dirty ass mattress wondering when security would be bringing me some sheets, a toothbrush, toothpaste, and toilet paper for this cell. I heard keys coming down the hall and saw the beam of a flashlight dancing on the hallway walls. I heard a steel door open, and slam shut then more movement headed down the cell block in my direction. The big cross-eyed sarge stopped at my door and said, "Remain on your bunk." He opened my cell door. Another officer walked up with an inmate, handcuffed behind his back. They pushed him into my cell.

I was like, *damn, it's way too hot back here to have a roommate.*

But I knew with the amount of people they would be locking up because of the riot, it might end up being three men to one small ass cell, built for two people. The third guy would have a mattress on the floor. If this inmate was one of them north Florida dudes, I was gonna beat his ass and put him on the door. I wasn't about to be in a two-man cell with an enemy – trying to sleep with one eye open.

The other officer was removing the handcuffs off my new cellmate. As my eyes adjusted to the darkness, I recognized who dude was. He had a slick ass mouth and was always talking shit anytime I saw him. I'm pretty sure we would be bumping heads in this little ass hot cell. He really couldn't see my face because of the angle I was laying down at, but I'm sure he could feel my eyes on him, sizing him up for whatever situation that may arise.

He spoke first, "Whassup with you, dude?"

I responded, making my voice deeper than normal. "I ain't friendly, so save all that conversation and get your ass on that top bunk, punk."

Dude was already getting in a defensive stance, with his back against the wall. I spoke once again, "I'm gonna need that breakfast tray in the morning also."

The dude responded, "The only thing you gon' get is fucked up back here trying to size me like I'm pussy."

I wait a few seconds and said, "You better be glad I know your mama, Cartoon, because if I didn't I'd break your neck back here."

He chuckled at that and said, "Country-ass Helimite! You need to stop playing them rock head games before you get faded back here."

"How am I country, Cartoon? You from Orange County. I'm from Palm Beach County. We have palm trees. Y'all have orange groves and Mickey Mouse."

He couldn't help but laugh at that one. I sat up, gave him a fist bump, and said, "Did Sergeant McMillen slap the shit outta you coming in?"

He shook his head, "Hell naw. I didn't even see his big silly ass."

"He slapped me, and I couldn't even duck it because I didn't see it coming."

Cartoon said, "Bro, they locking up just about everybody. Security trying to flip the population. Captain Zipper locked me up under investigation because I'm from Orlando and he said I looked like I'm guilty of something."

Captain Zipper never did like me even when I was across the street at the west unit. That was my first time ever seeing him. I probably need to let my hair grow back. They see a young black man with a bald head and automatically feel like I'm a troublemaker or in a gang when the truth of the matter is that just about every baller in college and the NBA right now has a bald head. Most of us incarcerated young ballers wore that look as well.

"I doubt we're gonna receive any of our property tonight, bro. They way too focused on just locking people up tonight. By 8:00 tomorrow morning, the A.C.I. snitch committee will have turned in a detailed list of who did what. So, relax, Cartoon. We both know you didn't put your hands or them batteries in the sock on nobody. You the Ivey lane Projects track star. One minute you was right next to me. I turned my head for a second and you was ghost."

"You had your pipe on you, Helimite. So, I wasn't gonna hold your hand going up the hill to the dorm. My lil homeboy Wayne didn't have a weapon to work with, so I handed him one of them thangs you gave me and we regulated our way back up to the dorm. It's quite a few cats back here in this Gator right now because of the knots me and Wayne put on their heads."

I nodded my head and listened to the details of their battle to reach the dorm. It was late and my body was starting to crash and shut down. I rubbed my jaw and could still feel the sting from that bitch slap Sergeant McMillen delivered. I guess it's safe to say, if the only harm I received out of this riot was one slap, I'll take that as a win-win, knowing God had kept me once again, in the midst of chaos.

CHAPTER 35

Seven whole days had went by and me and Cartoon was still on the dark side of The Gator. Security had decided not to issue us any of our property. All we had was a state-issued toothbrush and toothpaste, and one yellow bar of pride prison-made soap. The only bright spot in our stay so far was Hustleman. He worked on the confinement cart every lunch and dinner and he made sure me and Cartoon received two extra trays every meal along with all the end bread from all the loafs of bread that had been served back here. That end bread along with a cup of that city water coming out the sink kept us full every night.

We had already established our cell routine. We worked out every day, but we really went hard on Monday, Wednesday, and Friday because those were the only days we could actually take a cold shower. There was no hot water back here. "Hot water would be too much of a luxury," the big cross-eyed sergeant had said, as him and Sergeant Sheely, who was 6'6" ran the showers on those nights.

By rule, anyone coming out of their cell for anything had to be hand-cuffed behind their back. These two sergeants never handcuffed anybody on shower night. They would tell you to put your hands behind your back like we were cuffed and then they would escort the inmate to the shower. "You have five minutes to wash your ass," one of them would say. And they meant it. Nobody in their right mind was gonna try and buck these two sergeants because we all knew they were just looking for a reason to beat our ass.

The Classification Department was not visible at all during this phase of waiting on a transfer or possibly being released back to open population. Beach Boy and Bump City didn't get locked up, but Malik did. He was four cells down from us. It was Friday night. Everyone was showered and it was hot, dark, and boring. Me and Cartoon shared stories of our upbringing in two different hoods. Me at Stoneybrook and him at Ivey Lane. It's amazing at how much stuff you can get into as a juvenile, growing up in the hood. We both were very creative when it came to making money. We both influenced the mindsets of those we grew up with, either by action or words.

There are two groups of people in this world – the haves and the have nots. The more I didn't have, the more I was excluded, isolated, and out of the money loop that travels many different routes. To upgrade my situation I had to listen, learn, and more importantly watch because seeing is believing. I found several avenues that would hurdle me forward in life as long as I applied myself. My daddy always told me that that best way to get on your feet is to get off yo' ass.

The weekend flew by in The Gator and Monday was a welcome sight to see. Monday through Friday were the only days we could hope a Blue Bird prison bus had finally arrived to transfer us or that security would release us back into open population. The officers working in The Gator weren't giving us any information. We were being held hostage with no end in sight.

I was laying in my bunk, covered in sweat, listening to every sound my ears could detect. A rat was moving around on our cell floor, eating whatever crumbs we may have dropped on the floor. I heard keys and one of the C.O.'s walkie talkie sounding off, "10-4 sarge," down the cell block. I heard the officer's boots against the concrete and saw a beam of light coming from the flashlight they carried. It came to a halt at our cell door.

"Inmate Helimite," the C.O. yelled out loud and clear.

"Yeah," I respond.

"It's, 'yes, sir,' inmate."

"Well, yes, sir, then," I barked back.

"Get up and get dressed in Class A uniform," the C.O. ordered.

"Am I transferring?" I asked.

"No, you're not."

"Well, where am I going?" I asked, curious about what I should anticipate.

"Mental Health," he responded.

I repeated, "Mental Health?

Cartoon sat up on his bunk and said, "I knew your ass was crazy, Helimite," and cracked up laughing while I proceeded to get dressed.

"Everybody has a lil crazy in them, Cartoon. Some of us just hide that crazy better than others."

The officer ordered Cartoon to remain on his bunk. I backed up to the door so they could handcuff me with my arms behind me. They opened the cell door, grabbed me by my arm and pushed me against the wall to add a pair of leg shackles. We begin walking down the cell block. Every inmate in The Gator is at their cell door trying to see who was going somewhere and why. I approached Malik's cell and all 6'8" of him was standing at his door with a t-shirt tied around his head like a du-rag. He saw me and his eyes widened. "What's up gangster?" he said.

"Mental health evaluation, Malik."

Before I can say another word, Cartoon yells out, "They wanna know why you haven't been taking your medication, fool."

The whole cell block erupted with laughter and humor.

I hollered back, "Whatever, Cartoon," and kept it moving.

I was escorted to a room with one window, a table, and two chairs. This room was normally used for disciplinary hearings, but today was different. The officers opened the door for me, and there she stood with that hourglass figure, afro picked out to perfection, with a blue pants suit on and white heels, white earrings, and a matching pearl necklace with a fragrance on that smelled amazing. She had, what appeared to be, my mental health file in her hand.

She spoke first, "Good morning, Helimite. Have a seat, please."

I sat down and the two officers escorting me backed up against the wall. The doctor acknowledged both officers and said, "You guys can wait outside. I will let you know when I'm done with this evaluation."

The officers looked surprised and one of them asked, "Are you sure?"

Dr. White responded, "No. I'm not sure. I'm positive that you two correctional officers need to remove yourselves due to everything that the inmate and I are about to be discuss is confidential and protected by HIPAA laws."

They stepped out in a hurry. Once the door closed, she opened my file, picked up her pen, wrote down something, looked at me and said, "So,

Mr. Helimite. I was absent for two weeks. I come back to work to hear that a riot had taken place and to find out that you were in lock up because of it."

I looked into her eyes and said, "I'm being held back here under investigation, Dr. White. If I had done something wrong, I would have been written a disciplinary report."

She stared back, clicking her ink pen, never breaking eye contact. "So, you are innocent?"

"I didn't say I was innocent. I said, 'I'm under investigation.'"

She bit down on her bottom lip, shook her head from left to right, and mumbled something I couldn't quite make out and then she began to ask all the professional questions. The first one was, "Have you been hearing any voices lately?"

"Yes, Dr. White, I have. Along with bad dreams as well."

"Really?" she asked. "Tell me about the bad dreams."

I responded, "It was all good lovemaking going on until she decided to give me an unexpected golden shower."

Dr. White sat back and said, "As in urine all over you?"

"Yes, Dr. White. She pissed all over me."

Dr. White leaned back in her chair and began to laugh. Once she stopped laughing, she explained to me that nine times out of ten, that wasn't urine, it was female ejaculation, also known as squirting.

I tried to take in all the information humbly because I just didn't know. I asked, "How should I interpret this dream, Dr. White? I heard every dream you have has a meaning or message for you to take heed to."

She answered, "From what you have told me, Helimite, you apparently was doing something right and hitting all her right spots to get that kind of reaction from her body."

I nodded my head.

She flipped a page in my file and asked, "Is your emergency contact still Dorothy Mae Jones, Mother, phone number 561-842-7122?"

I confirmed the information.

Dr. White continued, "Is Teresa Ward, Sister, phone number 561-844-9103 your other emergency contact still, and are both numbers still the same?"

"Yes, Dr. White. Those numbers should never change."

"I'm in the process of closing out your file here at Apalachee Correctional Institution since you will be transferring to Jackson Correctional Institution tomorrow."

I mumbled, "Jackson? Where is that?"

"About an hour north of here," she answered.

"So, I guess this is goodbye, Dr. White?"

"Not necessarily, Helimite. I plan on starting a private practice in Houston, Texas in a few years. Whenever you get out, I will be listed in the Yellow Pages should you need my mental health services."

I nodded my head and said nothing. In that moment, I just wanted to take her all in. I took mental pictures to remember how she looked and acted on this last evaluation. I finally found my words and said, "I appreciate everything you have done for my mental state of being while I was here. I'll never forget it. I will keep you and your family in my prayers always."

She stared back at me with a sad look on her face and said, "When you get out of prison, Helimite, you will make some young lady extremely happy, somewhere in this small world of ours."

At that point, she stood up, gathered her file and walked out the door. I watched her swing that big ass from left to right as she departed. The voice in my head finally decided to speak. *Helimite, that woman is a whole damn brick house.* I answered out loud, "She sho' is."

The two officers entered the room, got me up, and escorted me back through the maze and back to my cell. They had Cartoon get back on his bunk and they removed the shackles from my legs in the hallway then opened the door and pushed me in. With my back to the door, I inched closer to it and let them remove my handcuffs. I could hear someone walking up but couldn't see who it was.

To my surprise, it was the big, cross-eyed sarge. He addressed the two officers, "Go get that food cart from the kitchen." They left immediately.

Sarge turned and looked into our cell. "Inmate Helimite."

"Yes, sir, Sarge," I answered.

"My cousin, Officer Bell, told me what you did for her. I wish she would have told me sooner. I wanted to tell you thank you from me and her. I spoke with Classification and asked them not to send you to F.S.P. Florida State Prison, which is where the majority of these inmates are going. Take care of yourself and stay up."

"Alright, Sarge. I appreciate that," I said. Sarge gave me a fist bump through the bars.

Cartoon was on the top bunk looking like, *is this negro snitchin' or what?* "What the fuck goin' on, Helimite? I ain't never seen Big Sarge act like that."

I took a deep breath and exhaled. "Cartoon, during that riot all kinds of shit was going on but hold that thought for a minute. I'll be transferring tomorrow to Jackson Correctional Institution."

"How you know that?" Cartoon asked.

"The mental health lady told me. Get something to write with and some paper before I forget." I gave Cartoon my mama's information, and I grabbed my Bible and wrote down his mama's information.

Cartoon asked, "Why you wrote it in your Bible, Helimite?"

I answered, "When I get released from prison, this Bible is the only thing I'm not giving away or leaving behind, bro. It's a sword, Cartoon, to gather wisdom from and to live by, if I can ever completely humble myself to do it. These cats in here be trying stuff, thinking you soft when they see you trying to live right."

Cartoon said, "It's too many cats that *hate* me for me to be trying to live holy up in here."

"They *hate* you, Cartoon, but they *respect* you at the same time. So, what that make you? *Respectfully Hated*, my brother. Just like me. *Respectfully Hated*."

A short moment of silence passed between us, and I continued, "From this point forward, I am no longer calling you Cartoon. I feel like your nickname may mislead people into thinking you a joke or clown ass dude, and they may end up getting they head split judging you on that nickname."

I repeated his nickname, "Cartoon," and paused. "From here on out Imma call your ass Toon, and you should have everybody else address you as Toon as well, my brother. Food for thought. The rest is up to you."

Toon looked at me and said, "You swear you got game, Helimite."

"I keep tryna tell you, bro. I'm official just like the referees."

"So, what Big Sarge was talking about you did for Ms. Bell?" Toon asked.

"I stopped three inmates from raping Ms. Bell during the riot. I *hate* to see or even hear about a man putting his hands on a woman. I was raised by women, and I have four sisters. I've seen some things in my lifetime that triggers me, Toon."

"What you mean, Helimite?"

"Listen to this true story I'm about to tell you."

CHAPTER 36

"Leave my mama alone," I screamed at the top of my young lungs.

"Take your li'l ass to you your room before I plant my foot in your ass next."

"You better not touch my son, Deion!"

"Bitch, shut up!"

Deion was my mama's boyfriend. He grabbed her by the throat then delivered a slap that sounded like a firecracker inside the small two-bedroom apartment that we had in Cocoa Beach. Deion then punched my mama in the stomach, knocking the wind out of her. She fell on the bed.

He screamed, "Breathe, bitch! Don't die on me now! Breathe!" Deion took off his shirt, laid on top of my mama and said, "You know I love you, Dot! You made me act like this tonight. Now get out them clothes. Dry up them tears and gimme the lovin' you know I deserve."

My mama didn't move or say a word. Deion slapped her again while on top of her, grinding against her, mumbling words I couldn't hear or understand. It was 1976. I was only eight years old, and my mama was hurting and in a lot of pain. I had to do something to help my mama. I grabbed the iron off the ironing board, eased back into that bedroom and swung that iron with all my eight-year-old might. It connected with Deion's head, splitting it and sending blood every which way. Deion screamed like a white woman in one of those creature-feature scary movies I used to watch on T.V.

I took off running out of the front door. I ran to one of my mama's friend's apartment and banged on the door. I told Ms. Gladys what had happened. She grabbed the biggest butcher knife I had ever seen out of her kitchen drawer. She locked me inside her apartment and went to go help my mama. I picked up her phone and dialed the only number I knew, my daddy. He answered the phone, and I told him what happened, and he said he was on his way.

I heard an ambulance in the distance. It was getting louder and louder as it arrived at the apartment I lived at. I looked out of Ms. Gladys's window, hoping my mama was okay and hoping Deion was dead just like all the bad people on T.V. ended up being dead. Dead. Gone forever. Ms. Gladys came back with a police officer. He asked me what had happened and wrote it all down on some paper.

I asked the police, "Is he dead?"

"No, young man. He is not dead, but he will need a lot of stitches."

"What is stitches?" I asked.

"It's when a doctor sews something back together that splits open. How did you know to pick up something to hit him with?"

"My daddy always told me if somebody bigger than me is trying to fight me, to pick up something hard and try to bust they head to the white meat."

The officer's walkie-talkie was loud. Somebody was asking him if he had a statement yet. He responded, "10-4." He looked at me and said, "I *hate* that's what your daddy always told you, but I *respect* what you did to Deion tonight. He had it coming. I just never thought it would come from an eight-year-old kid," and he turned to leave.

"Where's my mama, Ms. Gladys," I asked.

"She's okay. I'm gonna walk you back over there."

As I got closer to the apartment, I see my daddy talking to my mama. I overheard him telling her, "Deion is a woman-beater. He beat every girlfriend he has ever had. You need to leave him alone. And if he put his hands on my son, I'm gonna put some hot lead in him. I'll help you change your locks in the morning, Dot."

My daddy looked at me and said, "Come here, son." He gave me a hug and said, "Call me if you need me. If that nigga Deion try to put his hands on you, let me know."

I responded, "Okay," and I hugged my mama who had blood stains all over her clothes. "Mama, you okay? You was bleeding?"

She shook her head and said, "No. This blood came from Deion's head. My son, you are way before your time. It's almost like you have been here before. Deion is gonna **hate** you for the rest of his life but he gon' *respect* you all at the same time. My baby boy will always be ***Respectfully Hated***.

I'm so glad you had the opportunity to read my books
before you passed. Even though you're gone,
you will live forever in my books.
Rest In Heaven, Nicole Ventress

Cartoon | Helimite

Knowing the value of your freedom is everything!

FREE AT LAST
FREE AT LAST
NO MORE SHACKLES
IT'S ALL IN THE PAST

CARTOON
IG: @407TAKERS

HELIMITE
IG: @HELIMITE1025
FB: @VINCENT.MCDANIELS

Cartoon and Helimite with Edgerrin James, NFL Hall of Famer & Host of the Create The Life Podcast.

Create the Life

The greatest gift of all is your time you are given, especially your present time. Make the most of it regardless of where you are at in life or on the earth.
-Toon

CREATE THE LIFE YOU WANT TO LIVE

Rufus | Helimite | Freddy J | Ant
The crew from the Laundry Memory at the end of Chapter 14

Helimite | Kearns

Books by Vincent McDaniels
Available now on Amazon.Com

Coming Soon

#4 In It To Win It
#5 Only On The Muck
#6 Links, Ties & Affiliations

www.ingramcontent.com/pod-product-compliance
Lightning Source LLC
Chambersburg PA
CBHW050407030726
47503CB00006B/2067